SEARCHING FOR STORMI (SPECIAL FORCES: OPERATION ALPHA)

FALLPORT RESCUE OPERATIONS

BOOK FOUR

JEN TALTY

Dear Readers,

Welcome to the Special Forces: Operation Alpha Fan-Fiction world!

If you are new to this amazing world, in a nutshell the author wrote a story using one or more of my characters in it. Sometimes that character has a major role in the story, and other times they are only mentioned briefly. This is perfectly legal and allowable because they are going through Aces Press to publish the story.

This book is entirely the work of the author who wrote it. While I might have assisted with brainstorming and other ideas about which of my characters to use, I didn't have any part in the process or writing or editing the story.

I'm proud and excited that so many authors loved my characters enough that they wanted to write them into their own story. Thank you for supporting them, and me!

READ ON!

Xoxo

Susan Stoker

To Kimberly. Had it not been for you, I would have never made it through this one! Thanks for all that you do.

CHAPTER ONE

Lincoln Walsh stared at the text message. His gut recoiled, and his heart turned black.

Sometimes he resented the sense of loyalty that had been ingrained in his brain. Otherwise, he would have quit two months ago.

But he couldn't do that. He'd fulfill his contract. Not that he owed his ex-girlfriend anything, but he did owe it to himself and his future.

Thank God for Fallport Search and Rescue. If he hadn't accepted a second job, he'd surely lose his fucking mind.

He snagged his rucksack, tossed it over his good shoulder, and winced as a sharp pain registered in his brain. He did his best to ignore what the doctor had told him would eventually become a dull ache.

It had been a year since he'd been shot. Wasn't that enough time?

He made his way from the baggage claim to the airport pickup. Stepping outside, the humid summer air smacked his skin like the thick fog that often hovered over London.

Sweat beaded across his forehead like water dripping from a leaky faucet.

He welcomed the change both in location and in climate. Lord knew he needed to do something different with his life.

Glancing left and right, he scanned the row of cars for his buddy Talon, or as everyone called him, Tal. The last decade had been hell without that man. Lincoln had tried everything he could to survive without the one person who had believed enough in Lincoln to give him a chance when everyone else had turned their back.

"Over here, man." Tal waved his hand out of a big, fancy SUV—the kind that soccer moms drove.

Lincoln chuckled as he opened the back seat door and tossed in his bag, biting back a groan. Fucking physical therapist told him the pain was weakness leaving the body. Lincoln had half a mind to fly back to the UK and give that idiot some pain to contend with. "Hey, old man." He slipped into the passenger seat and gave his buddy a good manly hug.

Tal was more than a best friend. A brother-in-arms. Tal had been Lincoln's savior.

"You're looking a little crusty around the edges yourself." Tal eased out into traffic.

"You're the one who's fifty-something. I'm forty, so bite your tongue." Lincoln buckled up and prepared to be weirded out by driving on the wrong side of the road. While this wasn't his first trip to the United States, it always threw him that Americans chose to drive on the right side. "So, how's Heather and the kids? I can't wait to meet them."

"They're looking forward to checking you out too."

"How old are your kids now?"

"Marisa, the oldest, is sixteen. And Chad is thirteen."

Lincoln let that knowledge soak into his mind as he stared out the window at the thick lush greenery pronounced by the bright sun beating down on the earth with its intense rays. It seemed like just yesterday that the man—no, the legend—had informed Lincoln that he was leaving the Special Boat Service and moving to the United States.

That had been fourteen years ago.

But that had been the day that Lincoln lost his mentor. His best friend. And the last person he called family.

Perhaps that seemed dramatic, but Lincoln had no blood relatives left. He had no ties to the UK. Moving to the United States after his relationship with Samantha—and his employment with her company, CyberGuard Solutions—had gone sideways, was a no-brainer. Accepting a part-time position with Fallport Search and Rescue was exactly what he needed to get his head out of his ass and start his life over after losing the last thing that made him feel alive. "I can't believe you are responsible for two little humans."

"Not so little anymore." Tal laughed. "Marisa is giving Heather and me a run for our money. She's a good kid. Gets good grades and is on the soccer team at school. We're proud of her, but she's found boys. Or should I say, one found her and I can't even scare him off. The whole thing freaks me out because I remember being his age."

"You don't want to know what I was doing when I was that age." Lincoln's early childhood years, those that he could remember, were considered normal. He had two loving parents, although his memories of them were more like blurry visions since they died when he was six. After that, his life turned to shit. He moved from one foster family to the next, getting himself into the kind of trouble that should have landed him in jail. That was until he turned seventeen and met Tal. He changed everything for Lincoln.

"You say that as if I don't know." Tal turned and lowered his chin. "You crash-landed into that café I happened to be having coffee at with my girlfriend at the time. You had hair down to your shoulders. You wore more makeup than my daughter and you looked like you slept in a dumpster."

"I was ditching the police." Lincoln shook his head. "You were all decked out in your spiffy military uniform and told me to sit in that commanding voice you had. I'm not sure who I was more scared of. You or the cops."

"I still can't believe you joined the Royal Navy because I told you to."

"It was better than living on the streets, stealing food and hustling for money." Lincoln nodded. "I know I've said it before, but you saved my sorry ass, and you're doing it for the millionth time. So, once again, thank you."

"You really are a sentimental fool and I know you. You'll land on your feet." Tal pulled off the main drag and turned into a quaint neighborhood just outside of Fallport, which was like nothing Lincoln had ever seen. It was this tiny little town that reminded him of a movie set from the past where everything was happy and nothing bad happened. "I'm a little shocked you're doing this for Samantha, though."

"It's the only way she'll let me go early. Otherwise, it's going to be a clusterfuck and I don't feel like fighting that woman. It's not worth it." Lincoln raised his hand. "Honestly, I don't feel like talking about it right now. Maybe after I get settled and get a better handle on this job, though, even then, I can't bring you into the work."

"You always say that, then ask me weird questions." Tal smiled. "If I can be of assistance, in any capacity, I've got your back." Tal was one of the only people in Lincoln's life who had never betrayed his trust.

"Tell me about Chad. What's he like?" Lincoln opted

to shift the topic of conversation. He'd spent the entire flight going through data. His mind needed a rest.

"He's a unique kid," Tal said. "He likes to fish. Hike. All the outdoors stuff. But he'd often rather spend his days with his nose in a book. You'll get along with him just for that reason. Spends all day at the library, just like someone else I know."

Books had always been Lincoln's salvation. It started with his mother, who would read to him every day. When he went to his first foster home, his foster mother had a hoard of books and he would devour them to the point the system believed he lived in a fantasy world.

Maybe he did because the real world was a shitty place.

As he grew into a man, when he wasn't getting into trouble, he was reading whatever he could find. He didn't care what it was. Fiction, nonfiction, it didn't matter. He loved them all. Tal encouraged his thirst for knowledge and once Lincoln joined the military, and they pushed an education, he thrived in the environment.

But the military had a tendency to find that hidden talent and Lincoln had a big one.

"It sounds like Chad and I might be going to the library together because no matter how much intel I can find on the internet, books are sometimes better."

"My son has a crush on the newest librarian." Tal rolled the SUV to a stop in the driveway of a modest home. It was two stories and not exactly what Lincoln had expected. It was very suburban-like. Not what he was used to in the UK. "Now that it's summer and school is out, Chad wants to go to the library almost daily. We've never discouraged his love for books. I mean, that's a great thing to have. But summers past, he'd want to fish or hike as well. Now that Stormi moved to town, all Chad wants to do is hang out there with her."

"My first heavy crush was on my sixth-grade teacher. She was smoking hot. I'll never forget the day her boyfriend showed up with flowers and proposed. Totally burst my bubble, but he was a cool dude."

Stormi. Interesting name. And not common. Names had always intrigued him, partly because his parents had named him after Abraham Lincoln. Odd for a British family to do. They had no ties to America or the history that brought about Honest Abe.

Lincoln's dad was a history professor, and the Civil War intrigued him personally. Lincoln only knew this because of a few boxes of belongings that he'd managed to keep from his youth. Tucked inside were notes his father had written about America. About how strange it was to him that a nation so new—so driven to become their own country—would have such a great divide so quickly.

It made for fascinating reading.

"Dad!" A young boy came barreling out the front door, arms flapping wildly. "Could you please tell

Marisa that she and what's his name can't hog the television all day? I want to watch something."

"Welcome to the nuthouse." Tal laughed as he climbed from the driver's seat. "Chad, say hello to my buddy, Lincoln."

Chad skidded to a stop. The boy was scrawny and maybe five foot five. He had a lot of growing to do. Hell, Lincoln hadn't filled out until he hit twenty. "It's nice to finally meet you. My dad said you and he served in the UK together."

"We did." Lincoln stretched out his hand. "I've heard a lot about you."

"Chad, why don't you grab Lincoln's bag. He's going to stay with us tonight. His place won't be ready until tomorrow."

"Sure thing, but will you pleeeaseee talk to Marisa?" Chad said.

"I'll be sending Brad home and we'll be having dinner shortly. So, no television for anyone until after that."

"Then you should know they were making out on the sofa when Mom went to the store and it wasn't simple kissing. Tongues were involved and some serious—"

"That's enough, son," Tal said in a stern fatherly tone.

"Whatever." Chad flung the rucksack across his shoulder, nearly toppling over, before he raced off toward the house.

Tal leaned against the truck and sighed. "I'm not ready for this shit. I've tried talking to her about boys, but she threw back in my face that they talk about all that stuff at school and that she already knows, but she doesn't know anything."

"Come on, man. We thought we knew it all at her age and she's not a baby."

"We're guys. We spent our youth trying to get into young girls' pants." Tal pointed to the house. "That's my daughter. I have a million penises to worry about. It's totally different."

"They were kissing. A little heavy petting. It's nothing."

Tal punched him on his good shoulder. "If you ever mention heavy petting and *my daughter* in the same sentence again, I'll beat the shit out of you. She's sixteen. Barely a junior in high school. It's not even funny to joke about shit like that and if you start acting like my wife, reminding me that someday she's going to have sex, get married, and make me a grandpa, I will do more than kick your ass."

Just then a young girl appeared at the door. "He's lying, Dad." She leaned against the front porch railing. "Chad's just mad he lost when we did a coin toss over what to watch. It was fair and square. Ask Brad. You know he wouldn't dare lie to you. He's too scared you'll either tell his father or shoot him."

"Oh, the joys of parenthood," Tal mumbled as he pushed from the vehicle. "Where's your boyfriend?"

"Inside helping Mom set the table," Marisa said. "I asked if he could stay for dinner, but Mom said it was up to you."

"Of course she did." Tal pulled Marisa in for a hug and kissed the top of her head. "This is my friend, Lincoln."

"Is it true you saved my father's life once?" Marisa asked.

"I don't know about that, but your dad saved mine more than I can count." Lincoln smiled. "It's nice to finally meet you in person."

"You too." Marisa nodded. "Sometimes you're all my dad can talk about." She shifted her gaze. "Can Brad stay? For the record, there was no make-out session. Brad might have kissed me, but I'm allowed to kiss my boyfriend. I'm going to be seventeen. People kiss. It's not a big deal and that's all that happened. Chad's just being a jerk and it's not like he didn't kiss Suzie. We all saw that at the Fourth of July picnic."

"We're not having this conversation now and I'll think about it." Tal tucked a piece of the girl's hair behind her ear. "Go inside and help your mother. I'll give you my answer shortly."

"Fine." Marisa turned, glancing over her shoulder. "We're all glad you're here. My parents have been looking forward to it. Oh, and I almost forgot. Mom invited Stormi for dinner. She thought it would be nice for Lincoln to know someone who loved books as much as he did and Stormi doesn't get out much. Actually, she's not sure she's ever seen her anywhere other than the library or the grocery store."

Lincoln swallowed. Meeting people wasn't high on his agenda. Especially women. One of the reasons he moved across the pond was because of the female persuasion. His last girlfriend turned out to be a class A bitch.

And he didn't call any woman that word.

But Samantha deserved it and then some after what she'd done.

"Well, shit," Tal said. "I told Heather not to go and do that on your first night, but I guess we both should have expected it after what she did when we came to London to visit, although she's been feeling horrible about how that turned out."

Lincoln rubbed the back of his neck, doing his best to compartmentalize his thoughts. While he'd only met Heather a handful of times, he loved the woman like a sister. She was the perfect partner for Tal. They complemented each other in ways that warmed Lincoln's heart. But this fucking matchmaker thing would be the death of him. "Yeah, that turned out to be pure hell."

"She had no idea Samantha would turn out to be a crazy person and break your heart."

"Samantha didn't break anything. If she had, I would have found a way to buy myself out of this contract." Only she'd destroyed his ability to trust anyone with breasts unless he already knew them and even that was a stretch. Not to mention how she rattled his ability to perform his job. "Besides, if this Stormi chick works at the library, then it's good I meet her, because I need to get a library card anyway and I wouldn't mind taking Chad there. That way Marisa and Brad can have some alone time." It was going to be too much fun to bust his buddy's chops about teenage love.

"You're a dick, you know that?"

"So I've been told." Lincoln crossed the threshold of his buddy's home. It smelled like homemade sourdough bread and red sauce. The living room was filled with family pictures and a few from Tal's days back in the UK. It screamed of family and good times.

Everything that wasn't Lincoln's life.

"The thing with Stormi is she's only lived here for two months and we've never seen her out with anyone. She doesn't seem to have any friends, and you know my wife. After some of the stuff she's been through, she wants people to interact with humans."

Oh boy, did Lincoln know that all too well. "As long as she's not trying to fix me up, and she's just being nice, I'll deal with it. But I'm not here to meet women. I need to do this one last assignment with CyberGuard Solutions and get Samantha out of my life for good."

"I get it." Tal nodded. "I will say I'm glad you're taking our local librarian joining us in stride."

"You might change your tune about that when I

make it clear I'm not interested to both her and your beautiful but meddling wife."

Tal slapped him on the back. "Stormi is a real looker."

"Don't care. I have three objectives. Finish this case. Work for search and rescue. And find a new fucking job. Not get involved. Those days are over." Thanks to fucking Samantha. What a lying, conniving, backstabbing woman she turned out to be. "But I promise to be nice about it."

"Good, because for a second there, you sounded like a bitter old man."

"I'm not bitter. I've just learned that I enjoy living alone. I like my space and I'm not willing to share."

"I have so much to say to that, but I will refrain," Tal said as he entered the kitchen.

"Lincoln. Aren't you as handsome as ever." Heather set something on the counter and raced over, giving Lincoln a massive hug. "How was the flight?"

"Uneventful. Just the way I like it." Lincoln kissed her cheek. "Thanks for letting me crash here tonight."

"I wouldn't have it any other way." She smiled brightly. "You've met the kids, but this young man is Brad, our daughter's boyfriend."

"I've been listening to stories about you for weeks." Brad stuck out his hand. "Did you really take a bullet for Mr. Ross?"

Lincoln waggled his finger in the direction of Tal. "You're telling tall tales again, I see."

"Am not. That's exactly what happened." Tal ducked his head in the fridge and pulled out two beers, handing one to Lincoln. "If this man hadn't shoved me out of the way, I'd be dead. Honestly, half our team would have died on that mission if it weren't for Lincoln. He's a true hero."

"I was simply doing my job and you would have done exactly the same thing." Lincoln took a massive swig of his cold one. He hated this conversation. He'd been all of twenty-three years old when that mission went sideways. That marked the first time he'd been shot and that bullet tore through his body like a lightning bolt. Lincoln honestly believed he was going to die that day, and the truth of the matter was that Tal dragged his sorry ass to the chopper, saving his life.

But it was Lincoln who received a medal for his heroism.

"Why don't we leave it at both of you saved each other," Heather said. "Otherwise, all we're going to end up listening to is both of you downplaying what you have done in your collective careers." Heather went back to setting things on the table. "Did Marisa ask you about Brad staying for dinner?"

"Nothing like putting me on the spot." Tal sighed. "In front of everyone."

Heather leaned closer to her husband and whispered something in his ear.

Tal closed his eyes for a brief moment and nodded.

"All right. Brad can stay, but he's on dish duty with Marisa."

"I don't mind," Brad said. "Thank you, sir."

"Come on, Lincoln. Let me show you to your room." Tal waved his hand. "We've got one guest room down here. Follow me."

Lincoln did as instructed. "Not my business, but I'm curious. What did Heather say to make you cave so quickly about letting Brad stay?"

Tal leaned against the dresser. "He and his dad just moved here a few months ago. His folks are going through an ugly divorce. We learned that his mom cheated on his dad and when she left, she walked away from her kid too."

"That's cold."

"She comes around every once in a while and takes Brad for a few days. Heather mentioned that was supposed to be this weekend."

"What happened?" Lincoln asked.

"I guess she decided to go off with her new boyfriend, assuming his dad would be able to take him and just left him at his dad's doorstep earlier today. I knew Norman went to a trade show with his company, Zero Gravity. The boy's seventeen. He can be alone, but he shouldn't have to be. Not like that anyway."

"Jesus. That sucks." Lincoln could see the stress etched into Tal's face. It was the same look he'd seen when Tal decided to take Lincoln in after he damn near forced Lincoln to explain why he was hiding from the cops and his pathetic life story.

But now Lincoln felt as though he needed to add to that stress, considering.

"Heather told Norman that we'd keep him overnight. If they weren't an item, I'd have no problem with it. The boy needs people who give a damn in his life."

"What about his grandparents? Aren't they in the picture?"

"His father's parents are no longer living. His maternal grandparents live a few hours away and they have some important gala this evening, or so Heather was told. I guess Brad already called them."

"Well, fuck, that's just kicking a kid when they're down." Lincoln knew all too well what it was like to be shuffled around. "I can sleep on the sofa or go find a hotel."

"He'll sleep on the sofa where I can hear him coming up the stairs or Marisa coming down." Tal laughed. "We've had to do it before." He shook his head. "Norman seems like a good man and a great dad. It's a real shame what his soon-to-be ex-wife did." Tal arched a brow. "I don't know the details, but I guess it goes beyond cheating."

"Do I want to even ask what you know?"

"Honestly, I think it has to do with his company, which was started by his wife's father, David Caulkin."

Lincoln ran a hand over his face. His gut twisted

into a massive knot. He wished he could believe there was no way Samantha couldn't have known this juicy piece of information.

But the woman was damn good at her job. Maybe too good. And she didn't have scruples. At least not like Lincoln did.

"What's got you looking like you have to take a massive shit?"

"I'm beginning to wonder why this case was so important to land," Lincoln said.

"How so?" Tal cocked his head.

"I know this goes without saying, but this has to stay between us."

Tal blew out a long breath and nodded.

"Zero Gravity hired Samantha. She told me I deal with this, she'll tear up my employment contract." He held up his hand. "I do have that in writing."

"Good to know." Tal glanced over his shoulder. "What exactly were you hired to do?"

"A few things, but mostly I'm looking into an ongoing computer breach."

"Ongoing? That doesn't sound good and what exactly are we talking about? Does it have to do with the launch being pushed back? Do you believe it was an inside job? Are they suspecting Norman? He's not a coder. Or an engineer. He works in marketing."

"Norman is someone I want to speak with. He's divorcing the daughter of the founder of the company. He could have reason to hurt them," Lincoln said. "But to be honest, Zero Gravity is a little on the sketchy side."

"Why do you say that?"

"I've been hired to find out who hacked them, and if they are still being hacked, and yet my access to their systems right now is limited. I can't do my job if they are tying my hands." Lincoln raked his fingers through his hair. "Since the company headquarters is only a half hour from here, I'd appreciate it if you didn't tell anyone about my assignment. I don't even have a solid motivation much less a reason for the breach, other than the two things that were leaked, which did cause the company to have to postpone that launch."

"I won't say anything, but you should know that Norman is looking for a new job. He wants out. He doesn't want to be tied to his ex-wife or her family. He's shocked they haven't found a reason to fire him," Tal said with a furrowed brow. The same one he used to get when he wanted to ask a question that he might not like the answer to. "When did Samantha offer you this job?"

"Yeah, my mind had gone there too." Lincoln nodded. "I signed her standard five-year independent contractor agreement. When we broke up six months ago, she wasn't going to let me go. Not without a fight and I don't have the money to buy her out. I talked her down to working another two years, but it wasn't going to be in the United States."

"That happened when Zero Gravity hired her?"

"Sort of. In order for her to land the contract, she needed someone here. I offered her a deal she couldn't refuse because I can't stomach working with or for her anymore." Lincoln swallowed. He'd given Samantha five years of his life. He'd loved and supported her and worst of all—he invested in her start-up while he was still active duty.

He couldn't have anything to do with CyberGuard Solutions while he was still serving his country. That might have been seen as an act of treason, considering some of the jobs she took. Ethical hacking has a bit of shade associated with it, and he understood that when he gave his fiancée the money.

Only, he had no idea that he'd fuck her six ways to Sunday.

Then wash, rinse, and repeat another way.

"So, basically, you cut another deal for yourself." Tal arched a brow. "Does that include getting any of your money back?"

"This is a big job. It will be enough to get me started." Lincoln rested his hand on Tal's shoulder. "The important thing is she'll be out of my life, for good."

"Heather feels so bad about what happened. Samantha seemed like she checked all the boxes."

"She lied to all of us." Lincoln shrugged. "I don't blame Heather or you. I'm a big boy and I walked into that dungeon all by myself. It's about to be over. Once and for all."

Heather stuck her head in the bedroom. "Dinner's ready and Stormi's here."

Lincoln sighed. Time to be charming, but he'd have to let her down easy. He rounded the corner into the kitchen and the air in his lungs flew out like an exploding volcano.

Motherfucker.

Stormi looked an awful lot like Amanda Norris. Sure, Stormi's hair was much longer and darker, but no way could he mistake those bright-blue eyes.

This changed everything.

CHAPTER TWO

"Thanks for inviting me." Stormi August swallowed the thick lump in her throat as she glanced between Heather, Tal, and the hot stranger.

"We're so glad you could make it on such short notice." Heather handed her a glass of red wine. "This is Tal's buddy from the UK. He just moved here, and we thought the two of you would hit it off. He's a massive book lover, like you." She smiled wide as she raised her glass.

"Huge history buff, this one," Tal said. "Also fascinated with anything that has a motor, and I mean anything. He once took apart a golf cart engine for shits and giggles, but then couldn't figure out how to put it back together. Can't say I was too pleased about that one since it was only a couple of years old."

"But I did get it working again." Lincoln chuckled. It was deep and rich and sent Stormi's stomach on the kind of roll she could do without. The last man to turn her guts inside out turned out to be a royal asshole. Sadly, she hadn't known that about him until after she'd married the dipshit.

"That only lasted a couple of months until it crapped out." Tal leaned against the back deck railing. "Lucky for you I had no use for the stupid thing."

"Not to mention I got better at stuff like that and my ability to deal with electronics and gadgets came in handy on missions." Lincoln lowered his gaze and arched his brow. It was as if he was speaking in some secret silent code with Tal and that annoyed Stormi. She no longer had anyone she could communicate that way with. When she'd been a little girl, it had been her father. Years later, her ex-husband—though she wasn't sure he was legally her ex. She wasn't sure how that all worked.

But now, she had not a single person in her corner.

"I will give you credit for being a computer wiz." Tal nodded. "But you take engines apart, and you suck at putting them back together."

"These two could go at this all night." Heather laughed. "If they're not busting each other's ass about what they can't do, they're showing off all the places they got shot and who saved whose ass and when. They're weird like that."

"Not true and we all know Lincoln's the one who saved me." Tal pointed his finger at the door. "On that note, we should get inside and eat before my wife's cooking gets cold and the kids polish it all off."

The last thing Stormi wanted to do was play footsie with a sexy ex-military man with an even sexier British accent. She'd come to Fallport to find out what she could about Zero Gravity on a more personal level. There were enough people in this town who either worked for the company or used to work there that might give up a piece of juicy gossip that could lead her in the right direction. Currently, she had very little to go on. Every time she got into Zero Gravity's computer system and found something, it wasn't what she needed to prove they were responsible for her father's death.

The last time she went inside, someone chased her out. Someone who had some serious skills, and that scared her on a different level.

Stormi followed Heather, her husband, and the tall, handsome British man with the bluest eyes she'd ever seen inside.

The children had placed the food on the table and were already seated.

She'd spent a fair amount of time with Chad at the library. He was a polite teenager and had a thirst for knowledge. But he wasn't coming to the library these days for books. Nope. He was coming to see cute little Suzie who volunteered in the children's section.

Stormi had also met Marisa before, but this was the first time meeting Marisa's boyfriend. Nice young man, but still, this was not how she wanted to spend her time. She should be home, behind her screens, looking for the intel that might save her father's legacy.

But Zero Gravity wasn't the easiest company to hack into. So far, it proved harder than the FBI or the DMV, and she'd been able to infiltrate both their systems.

"This smells wonderful," Stormi said as she sat at the table next to Mr. Tall-Drink-of-Something. "I don't cook much. I mean, it sucks cooking for one." That, and she was the worst in the kitchen. If it required more than a microwave, it was above her ability, and even then that might be asking too much.

"I eat out, order in, make a sandwich, or go hungry." Lincoln raised his glass. He had short blond hair with a boy-next-door smile that made her insides sing like a canary. "The last time I tried to cook, I nearly burned down my kitchen."

"That's bull. You're an excellent cook." Heather passed a dish to the right. "Last time we were in the UK, Lincoln made us an amazing meal. But he's like you and doesn't really like cooking for one person." Heather tilted her head and gave Lincoln a sweet but sort of sad smile.

"Not entirely true." Tal laughed. "He can only manage about ten things in the kitchen and one of them is a chocolate cake, which is about the most amazing thing I've ever put in my mouth and I'm going to demand you make it for us in the near future."

"Oh, now that I can get on board with," Stormi said.

"Me too." Marisa reached across the table. "Can we take our food into the family room? It will give you adults time to be adults."

That caught a laugh from Tal.

"Only if you promise to be nice to your little brother." Heather waggled her finger. "And he gets to pick the show."

"I can live with that," Marisa said.

The three teenagers took their plates and raced off to the other room.

"Those are some well-behaved kids," Lincoln said.

"They have their moments." Heather sipped her wine. "Chad looks up to Brad and in turn, Brad likes the little brother, which can cause a different set of problems. But at least our kids aren't doing some of the stuff we did as children."

"Thank God for small favors." Tal dug into his casserole and stuffed it into his mouth.

Stormi had about as normal an upbringing as one could fathom. She was raised in Upstate New York where she wanted for nothing. As a matter of fact, her parents had been incredibly wealthy and lavished her with designer everything. Even after tragedy took her mother from her at the ripe old age of twelve, her dad managed to give her all the love in the world. While she missed her mom every day, her dad made sure she never went without his support.

But sometimes he went a little overboard as she was

never forced to work, but she did anyway. She liked making her own money, and she loved technology. So much so, that by the time she was sixteen, she found a way into her high school's computer system and changed her grades. Not that she needed to for most of them, but one tiny little C in English was bringing her down.

She didn't get caught that time, but at the age of twenty-seven, she found herself in a whole heap of trouble, though she wasn't the person responsible. That was the work of her husband, whom she helped send to prison.

Hence the reason she was even given the short leash she was on now with one particular FBI agent who believed her story about her father.

"So, Stormi, how long have you lived in Fallport?" Lincoln asked.

"Only two months." Obviously, Tal and Heather hadn't given him the lowdown. Perhaps he'd been ambushed as well since she knew absolutely nothing about him. "What brings you here?"

Lincoln glanced between Heather and Tal with that same damned arch brow and lowered chin, as if to communicate something she was not privy to. "I'm going to be working search and rescue with Tal."

"He's also a—"

"Let's not bore your guest with shop talk," Lincoln interrupted Heather.

"I'm certainly not bored. I understand many of the

search and rescue team members have a second career. What's yours?" Stormi should stop asking questions. That meant she was interested in him, and she certainly wasn't.

Okay, so he intrigued her on many levels, but as a man to date, or even have a fling with, absolutely not.

"I'm actually going to be between jobs soon as I finish up a contract with the company I've been working at for the last year in the UK." Lincoln shrugged. "I have a degree in computer science, so I'd like to find something in that field, but it wasn't my main focus in The Special Boat Service, and that skill set doesn't always look good on a job application."

"Now he's pulling your leg." Heather lifted the wine bottle and topped off everyone's glass. "He was Tal's intelligence officer when he was on his team. The man can hack into any system. He's super scary when it comes to computers and all that stuff. Tal once told me he watched him write code in the field so they could send encrypted intel back home. Tal described it as badass."

"You're talking way over this little librarian's head." Only every nerve ending in her body tingled out of excitement and a healthy dose of fear. Special Agent Kara Roger was the federal agent who had arrested her three years ago. Stormi could still feel the cold metal cuffs gripping her wrists. It was a sensation that constantly prickled her skin.

However, Kara was the kind of agent who listened

and looked at every detail. She left no stone unturned and she believed Stormi was innocent. A pawn in her husband's game. Kara presented Stormi with an out. Put Kurt in prison and then help her when she needed it.

Stormi didn't hesitate. The only negative was, she had to die in order to do it. That meant she couldn't reconcile with her father.

But she supposed that didn't really matter because he'd been too disappointed in her life choices anyway.

In the last three years, Stormi had used her computer savvy to aid Kara in three different cases. Honestly, it felt good. But when her father died, Stormi went right to Kara. At first, Kara advised her to stay out of it. She was too close and was supposed to be dead, but Stormi couldn't do it. She had to get her fingers inside Zero Gravity. When Kara found out, she'd been furious. Nearly hauled her in. But instead, she told Stormi she could poke around; she just couldn't leak any information.

But if the rocket ship was cleared for takeoff, that would mean more innocent people could die.

"How about we take this outside," Heather said. "It's a beautiful night. We might as well enjoy it. I'll get our dessert and Tal can wrangle the kids to start on these dishes."

"Sounds like a plan." Lincoln snagged the bottle, stood, and made his way to the sliding glass doors. "After you." He waved his hand.

Stormi would have a little more wine and then excuse herself. She did have to work in the morning, although the library didn't open until ten. But still, that would be her reason for a quick departure. She allowed Lincoln to refill her glass and she eased into one of the lounge chairs. "Look at that moon." She let out a long breath. The idea that all these companies like Zero Gravity were working toward making private spaceflight a possibility for the masses was something that still blew her mind. Flying wasn't something she enjoyed doing, so why on earth would she want to go to space for the fun of it?

"When I was a kid, I used to honestly believe it was made of cheese and all I wanted to do was find out what it tasted like."

She burst out laughing. "I'm sorry. But that has to be the dumbest thing I've ever heard."

"Sure, as an adult. But to a six-year-old with a very vivid imagination, it made perfect sense." He sat down next to her and pointed. "I mean, it kind of looks like Swiss. It reminds me of this book my mom used to read to me."

"Ah... *Mouse and the Moon Made of Cheese*. That's a popular one. It's read a lot during story time at the library."

"I have to ask. Is Stormi your real name? Or is it a nickname?"

"My real name," she said with a nervous laugh. It wasn't the first time someone had asked her that question in the last couple of years. But for some reason, it struck her as odd coming from this big, strapping, ex-military guy. Especially when no one else in this town had ever asked.

"Your parents must have had an interesting sense of humor."

"I don't know about that." She lifted her glass and took a slow slip. For months she'd rehearsed her back-story. Kara had quizzed her on it. It had become second nature. Only, she'd learned real quick that she didn't need to express it all that often. No one cared.

Especially when she didn't get out much.

"Although my mom did go into labor in the middle of a winter storm."

"Now it all makes sense." He chuckled, nodding his head. "How long have you been a librarian?"

Boy, was he full of questions and that was a loaded one, simply because she'd never actually been one. However, she did love books. She read at least one or two a week, but only because she didn't have a social life since she'd turned on her husband. Hell, she didn't have one during her marriage. All she did was work, read, and fiddle with all her gadgets. Technology was more reliable than people.

And that was a big oxymoron if there ever was one.

"It's what I went to school for, so since I was twenty-one." That was one big fat lie, but if he went looking into her background, that's what he'd find. She,

Kara, and a few highly qualified federal agents made sure of it.

"That really doesn't answer my question and forces me to either ask it again or ask you how old you are." He arched his brow and curved his lips into a half smile.

It was an adorable look on the Brit.

"I'm thirty." She chuckled. "And now it's your turn."

"Forty years young. Or at least that's what my brain says. The body, well, that's a different story." He took a long slow sip of his wine before glancing over his shoulder. "Do you think our hosts are ever coming back?"

"I hope so, because I don't want to be rude." She raised her glass. "When this is done, I will need to call it a night." Now she was going to have to set this gentleman straight. "I also feel like I need to take this opportunity to tell you that I had no idea anyone other than Tal and Heather would be here tonight. No offense, you seem nice enough, but I'm not looking to date anyone. I hope you can—"

"Let me stop you right there." He rested his hand on her forearm. "They didn't tell me you were coming either. I'm dealing with wrapping up with my previous employer. Looking for a new tech job, or maybe even starting my own. I also literally moved to a new country. Dating is the last thing on my mind. Not to mention, I'm six months out of a really shitty relationship. If you hadn't brought this up, I would have.

Heather means well, but this isn't her first time meddling in my love life."

"How has she done that? Because this is the first time she's tried to set me up." Stormi raised her hand. "No offense, but I hope it's the last."

"Knowing Heather the way I do, it's not really a blind date, but an introduction and the rest would be up to us."

"Now who's not actually answering the question." Her stomach hadn't filled with butterflies while talking with a man in years. If ever. Not even with her ex-husband. Her attraction to Kurt had been more about computers than sex. They spent their free time screwing around with coding and hacking more than they did in the bedroom. Her vibrator got more action than Kurt did, or so she thought.

It wasn't until Kara had arrested Stormi and showed her proof that her husband had been cheating, making it even easier for her to turn.

"I'd honestly rather not discuss my ex. It tends to put me in a sour mood," he said.

"I think we've all got someone in our past who has a tendency to do that to us." She clanked her glass against his. "So, who do you work for now? And what are you looking for in a new company? Or what kind of company would you start?"

"The firm isn't based here." He continued to stare at the moon. "Unfortunately, because of the nature of the work, I can't really talk about it. Tal knows that, but Heather doesn't. As far as the rest of it?" He shrugged. "I need time to settle into life here, and then I'll figure that out."

When she and Kurt started their cybersecurity company, they could never discuss the caseload. They signed NDAs for the firm and for each individual work order. So she understood Lincoln's position. Only, that made her more curious and terrified at the same time.

"I can understand, but I have to admit, all the talk about not being able to chat about it makes it all the more fascinating," she said. "Are you working on something now?"

"I can tell you that I am, but I can't say anything about it."

"I don't know much about computers, outside of how to use them on a base level." One of the hardest things for her to do was to keep things simple when talking about tech. Dumbing it down had always been damn near impossible. Acting as if she couldn't do something when it came to any computer system made her twitch, but she had to. No one could know who she really was or what she was doing. "I understand the library's system and I can help people navigate that and I know all the ebook readers and sort of how they work. Or at least I can troubleshoot them for people using Google."

That caught a good chuckle from Lincoln. "You

gotta love a good how-to video. That's how I figured out how to take apart an engine. Putting it back together, though, I tried to do that on my own and I was left with extra parts."

"That doesn't sound good."

"Nope. Especially when one of those parts goes to the brakes." Lincoln turned. "Tal left that part out of the story. When I finally got that damn golf cart working, I still had some spare parts. I took the whole thing apart again, and the next time, I was only left with two spare components. Since it started, we figured we were good to go. Tal crashed it into a light post, and then it rolled down a massive hill."

"That's what he meant by crapping out?"

Lincoln nodded. "I felt so bad because he broke his arm. He'll never tell the story that way for two reasons." He waggled his fingers. "My guilt and his."

"You're going to have to qualify that because it was an accident."

"That broken arm meant he was sidelined for a mission. One that went horribly wrong in so many ways. Not because he wasn't there, but he'll always wish he was and wonder if he would have done something different. I, for one, am glad he wasn't. He would have been point, and he would have died, since our point man did." Lincoln let out a long breath, lifting his shirt. "I took four bullets to the gut and nearly lost my life as well. I was only nineteen. Tal felt more responsible for what happened to me because of that stupid golf cart, which was my fault to begin with."

"I'm sorry, I don't understand. Besides Tal being the one who brought up the story, I don't get why he'd feel responsible, and you're still vertical."

Lincoln burst out laughing. "That's one way to look at it." He cleared his throat. "The thing is, Tal pushed me off that cart right before it rolled over on his arm. He'll always believe if he hadn't done that, I wouldn't have nearly died because I might have broken something too. There are so many what-ifs, but to truly understand the dynamics between us, you have to go back to when we first met. You see, Tal and I met when I was seventeen. I was living on the streets. He took me in, talked me into joining the Royal Navy, and has this weird older brother-father thing with me. I totally appreciate and value it, because Lord only knows what would have happened to me if I hadn't stumbled into that café that day." Lincoln pressed his finger over her lips when she opened her mouth. "He saved my life. Literally. But he'll tell you I gave him purpose. So, when they came to him and told him I'd been mortally wounded and probably wasn't going to make it, I guess he lost his shit."

"What happened still isn't his fault."

"He knows that. And so do I. But it all boils down to every other time one of us got shot or injured, one of us had to drag the other to an evac point. We joke sometimes that we were put together to have each other's backs. And we did. It was a damn hard day for me when he left the UK Boat Service and moved here."

"I imagine it was."

"If I had my time in, or was ready, I would have left with him. To be honest, he's the reason I took the job with search and rescue here and moved across the pond." Lincoln rubbed his shoulder. "It's kind of sucked the last fourteen years without him."

"That's a sweet story," she said.

He waved his wine. "Only told it because I've had one too many of these. I'm more of a whiskey drinker and this stuff just makes me sappy and loose with the lips."

She found herself leaning closer. "If I fed you more, would you talk about your work? Because I find it utterly fascinating." Her heart hammered in her throat. Someone new had been lurking in the digital halls of Zero Gravity. Someone professional. Someone who knew exactly what they were doing.

Someone like her, and she needed to know if that person was Lincoln.

"Nope." He set his glass down. His hot breath tickled her lips. His fingers danced across her biceps. "But it might make me do something crazy, like call off my dating rule." He ran his thumb over her cheek.

She swallowed. Hard. Her eyes locked with his dark orbs, totally mesmerized by his intense gaze. She needed to pull away. Attraction was one thing. She saw good-looking men daily. This town was full of them.

But they didn't affect her the way Lincoln did.

"Definitely not a good idea," she whispered.

"You're right." He leaned back, resting his head on his hand, shifting his stare back to the sky. "You're an incredibly attractive woman who can carry a conversation. A breath of fresh air. I want to get to know you better. Would you be up for a cup of coffee sometime?"

"That sounds like you're asking me out on a date." As much as that wouldn't be a good idea, she needed to learn more about his other job. About his skills. About what he was really doing in Fallport.

He turned and smiled. "No. Just two people getting together and perhaps chatting about books. A date would be if I asked you to dinner and I don't know you well enough for that. Maybe in the future."

She cocked her head.

He lifted his hands. "Coffee. Just coffee. I swear."

"I'll think about it." She glanced over her shoulder. "Heather and Tal are not coming back out here. As a matter of fact, they are both watching us."

"I noticed that ten minutes ago."

She stood, smoothing down the front of her jeans. "Time for me to go say goodbye. It was a pleasure meeting you."

"Are you okay to drive?" He rose and opened the sliding glass doors that led to the kitchen.

"I've only had two glasses. I'm fine."

"All right. Get home safely." He kissed her cheek. "I look forward to seeing you again."

Now all she needed to do was get Lincoln talking and pretend like she was dumber than a doornail.

Yeah, that should be easy enough.

Not.

CHAPTER THREE

Lincoln leaned against the deck railing and sipped his bitter brew. The nice thing about coffee was that in most places, coffee was coffee. It tasted the same no matter where he went.

Only, this morning, he needed a double shot of caffeine.

He'd spent half the night going down a new rabbit hole and didn't like what he'd found.

Someone had done an excellent job of making Stormi look like something she wasn't to the untrained eye.

But Lincoln was the best of the best. He knew only two other men who could potentially beat him at his own game.

Darius Ford and Wyatt Bixby.

Both men worked for the Brotherhood Protectors

organization. One out of the Colorado branch and the other in the Yellowstone office.

"Waking teenagers during the summer is never fun." Tal stepped outside and handed Lincoln a warm chocolate croissant. "Brad was easy, but the poor kid is feeling displaced and, frankly, unloved by his mother. He's not a child, but he's not a man."

"I know that feeling." Lincoln stuffed half the treat into his mouth and let the chocolate settle on his tongue while his taste buds exploded. He took a moment to gather his thoughts, which were a jumbled pile of mismatched information that he had no idea how to file. "You're doing the right thing by supporting and giving him a safe place to land. He seems like a decent boy with a good head on his shoulders."

"He is. And he's smart too. He wants to go into the Air Force Academy. I wrote a letter of recommendation, and he got a congressional nomination. His grades are top-notch. I'm sure he'll have no problem getting in."

"You sound proud."

"I kind of am, but then I worry about Marisa. I'm not blind. But they are too young to be so attached. He's the first boy she's ever really dated, and sadly, he's exactly the kind of young man I want her to be with. But not at fucking sixteen. I don't want her falling in love at that age."

"Unfortunately, first loves don't always last."

Lincoln set his mug on the railing. "We all have to have our heart broken at least once."

"I don't want my little girl ever to go through that."

"It might not be her who gets her soul crushed." Lincoln cocked his head. "And from where I'm sitting, it sounds more like you're the one who's worried about giving that kid up."

"Now you sound like my wife."

"Speaking of Heather, I need you to do me a favor," Lincoln said.

Tal raised his hand. "I had nothing to do with last night and I've already asked Heather to stop playing matchmaker, to which she scowled and informed me that's not what she was doing. She feels like Stormi hasn't made any connections and she knows how you get when you're working and sulking."

"I'm going to ignore the comment about my demeanor." Lincoln shook his head. "But that's not what I was referring to. I need her not to mention my other job. I can't have anyone in this town know who I work for. While both Samantha and Zero Gravity are keeping it in the vault, I can't afford for it to get out."

"I mentioned that too, and she gets it, but she's now worried about how this will affect Brad and his father."

"I understand her concern."

"What can you tell me about what you have on Norman? If anything."

Lincoln raked his fingers through his hair. He'd only been working on this case for five days. During that time frame, he'd learned very little, other than whoever leaked the information regarding the potential problems with the rocket launch wasn't done yet. Lincoln knew that because right before he'd boarded a plane, he came face-to-face with the hacker inside the computer system and he had to admit, whoever this person was, they were good.

But he suspected that person wasn't Norman. At least not in the flesh. But that didn't mean he hadn't hired someone.

"He's got motivation for revenge," Lincoln said.

"Once you meet him, you'll figure out real quick, he's more relieved his marriage ended than pissed. His only concern is how it affects his son moving forward."

"Maybe so, but that doesn't change the fact his wife cheated on him with a colleague and someone he considered a friend. His life has been turned upside down and he's out a shit ton of money. Not just by divorcing, but if he leaves Zero Gravity, he loses his stock options, among other things." Lincoln held up his hand. "I don't care what anyone says, money always makes people do weird shit, me included. However, Norman doesn't have the computer skills to do what I've seen. He'd have to hire someone and while it's been believed it was someone from the inside, I'm not so sure about that."

"What makes you think that?"

"I'm not prepared to express my thoughts just yet." Lincoln lifted his coffee and downed the last few gulps while he organized all the information and contemplated his approach to the next part of this conversation. It could have the potential to start a fight.

Something he didn't want.

"To be honest, while Norman makes sense on a motivational standpoint and on paper, my instincts tell me he's not worth my time and energy." Lincoln folded his arms across his chest. "My bigger issue now is Stormi."

"Why do you say that?" Tal narrowed his stare as he rested his hip against the railing. "How is she involved in this? And don't go giving me half answers."

"I can't tell you everything, but I can tell you, Stormi isn't who she claims to be."

"What the fuck does that mean?"

"For starters, she's not a librarian and her real name isn't Stormi." Lincoln leaned over and snagged the file on Stormi from the table. He handed it to Tal, going for broke. If he could trust anyone, it was Tal, and right now, Lincoln didn't trust himself. "This is what I needed your printer and privacy for this morning. I've highlighted what I'm willing to share with you, but remember—"

"Yeah. Yeah. I can't repeat it. I think you're forgetting who you're talking to." Tal eased into one of the chairs in front of the small table on the deck. He flipped open the folder and lifted the color-coded paper. "Do I need to be worried about my family's safety?"

"From Stormi? I don't believe so." Lincoln stared out across the yards and rubbed the back of his neck. After Tal had left the Special Boat Service, Lincoln had found himself at a crossroads. Missions just weren't the same without Tal. Nor was the team. That's when Lincoln had gone into a more specialized position, hanging back and working intel from a different vantage point.

However, he still went on missions, and the last one made it clear that it was time to retire.

But he'd also fallen head over heels in love with Samantha. While sometimes he hated to admit that, it was still the truth. After he retired, instead of moving to the States, like originally planned, he opted to propose and settle into life with a woman whom he honestly didn't know that well, even after five years of dating, and a few years of living together.

Something that still affected his ability to trust his instincts about anyone.

"Dante Norris?" Tal glanced up and blinked. "I remember that story. He was an engineer for Zero Gravity. He worked on the rocket boosters. The ones that exploded. He died a year ago while they were doing some test. I believe he was ultimately blamed for the explosion. But I don't get the connection."

"He was held responsible." Lincoln nodded. "After an internal investigation, the company made a statement that Dante cut numerous corners to bring new technology to the rocket before any other private spaceflight company. According to Zero Gravity, Dante had hopes of not only making a name for himself, but potentially selling the tech to other spaceflight companies as well as the government." He tapped the paper. "It was all backed up by an independent study, as well as an FBI probe. But get this." Lincoln reached in front of Tal and yanked out the last piece of paper. "Special Agent Kara Martin stuck her nose into this investigation, even though it wasn't hers. She dug in places that her bosses thought went a little overboard."

"But in the end, the FBI signed off on it." Tal waved a piece of paper. "Says so right here, and until the leak a month ago, Zero Gravity was back in business."

Lincoln shrugged. "Zero Gravity completely cooperated. They gave the Feds all the pertinent information. The FBI had full access to Dante's research and testing. It all came down to Dante fucking up and being greedy. There was nothing the FBI could do but sign off."

"So what has your panties in a wad? And what does it have to do with our local librarian?" Tal sighed, pushing the documents aside and waving his hand over them. "I'm not going to read it. Your color-coding and bullet points give me a fucking headache." He leaned back and glared. "I've missed you, but not that shit."

"Now you really know how to hurt a man's feelings." Lincoln tapped his chest. "There's so much that bothers me about this case and I'm going down a rabbit hole that I wasn't hired for. I was to get in, find the hacker, close the breach, build a new system. Simple, right?"

"If you say so."

"I never intended to spend any length of time on this. I want out from my contract. I don't want to deal with Samantha for a second longer."

"I don't blame you there."

"David, Norman's father-in-law, believes it was an inside job. Someone loyal to David. He never once mentioned to me that Dante had a daughter. One that graduated top of her class with a computer science degree from MIT. Neither did Samantha, but I suppose it's possible she didn't know and she wouldn't have any reason to go looking for it."

Tal lowered his chin and sucked in a massive breath. "Well, now, that's damn fucking interesting. When did you learn this?"

"That's where it gets interesting. The daughter's name was Amanda Norris. She was arrested three years ago for using her cybersecurity company to help a couple of criminals launder money and a few other unsavory things."

"Okay. And?"

"Amanda and Stormi are the same person."

"What the fuck?" Tal blinked.

"Yup. Only I didn't put that together until last night and didn't prove it until this morning. Which means, our Stormi is about as good of a hacker as I am."

Lincoln scratched the side of his face. "Before I knew about Stormi and was doing a search on Amanda, I got what everyone else got. Amanda went to MIT. Became an ethical hacker. Got married. Got arrested for doing a bunch of shady shit with her husband, using the cybersecurity company they formed together."

"Jesus, that sounds a little too close for comfort."

"I know. But according to my research, Amanda died by suicide shortly after being arrested. According to the media, she was consumed by guilt for what she'd done." He raised his finger. "So, I focused on the husband, wondering if maybe if he had something to do with my hack."

"Isn't he still in prison?"

"Doesn't mean he doesn't have people on the outside or knew people inside Zero Gravity through his wife."

"Any chance Stormi is working with her husband?"

"That is doubtful." Lincoln cracked his knuckles. Something he did when he was a little too excited. "The FBI agent that arrested her and her husband also worked Dante's case, though it was on the very fringes of it." Lincoln pulled back one of the seats and plopped his ass down, exhausted from lack of sleep and staring at small portable computer screens. He couldn't wait to set up shop in his new home.

"Now that's incredibly interesting." Tal folded his arms. "Are we talking witness protection?"

"My guess is she's in WITSEC." Lincoln stretched

out his legs. "My friend Darius, over at the Brotherhood Protectors, his wife, Fenmore, is former FBI. She has some serious connections. I should have a better handle on what I'm dealing with when it comes to Stormi by the end of the day." He rolled his neck. "But since Stormi is Amanda, well, that presents a whole new set of problems."

"Because Amanda's supposed to be dead, and I take it her dick of a husband made some dangerous enemies."

"It goes beyond that. I have to be concerned that Samantha knew about Stormi."

"How? She landed in your lap, almost literally."

Lincoln nodded. "Of course, this isn't even the scope of what my company was hired to do. We're supposed to find the threat, close the hole, and make sure Zero Gravity doesn't have any more leaks while loading a new system. However, Samantha knows me. She knows I'm like a dog with a bone with stuff like this."

"What else aren't you telling me?"

"A lot. But you're going to have to trust me. I certainly don't want to expose Stormi's identity, but you should know that Zero Gravity has been a client of CyberGuard Solutions for four years."

"Excuse me?" Tal leaned back and folded his arms. "That you should have told me at the beginning of this conversation." He shook his head. "Why are you doing this job?"

"I almost backed out twice. But because Samantha never told me they were a client or that she wrote the security program—"

"Wait. How the fuck didn't you know that?"

Lincoln sighed. For a smart guy, Samantha often made him feel like an idiot. "You have to remember, I worked for her. It was her company." He held up his hand. "Yes. I was an unofficial investor, which fucked me in the end. But she assigned the workload. I didn't pay attention to what she or anyone else did. And when I caught her fucking Tony on my desk, I walked out and actually never returned to the office. I went back to our apartment, collected my things, and moved in with Bernard."

"He's a good man."

"That he is." Lincoln nodded. "Of course, after I licked my wounds, I found out all the other shit that she did. But I don't want to dwell on that. I don't believe it has anything to do with this problem. However, I'm a little beyond fascinated by what I've uncovered since I've gone poking around in places I'm not supposed to. Zero Gravity might be slightly sketchy."

Tal jerked his head. "Seriously? If it's sketchy, and she installed their security system, she is the problem."

Lincoln laughed. "She wouldn't have me poking around in there, finding her mistakes, knowing I would, if she were trying to cover something up."

"Unless she wanted you to take the fall for something."

"But what? Because I've considered that too." Lincoln pursed his lips. "I know she's got all sorts of issues and addictions. It was easy for her to hide them from me when I was deployed all the time. I have to wonder if she didn't want to get caught, but that's not the point. CyberGuard Solutions is in financial trouble. She needs this. I know she'd like me to stay on. She's even offered to have me run an office here in the States. There's a small part of me that believes that's why she was trying to hold me to my contract."

"That's possible." Tal nodded. "But I don't like coincidences, and they are piling up like flies on shit."

"That's why I'm going to stall for a bit."

"That's a dangerous game where your ex is concerned," Tal said. "Stormi took one big risk the moment she moved this close to Zero Gravity's headquarters," Tal said. "Her father's worked for that company for years."

"Ah, but Amanda-Stormi hasn't had a relationship with her old man, at least not a good one, since she was twenty years old. I bet not a lot of people would recognize her. Hell, if it weren't for those damn gorgeous eyes, I wouldn't have. And let's be honest about that. It's always the eyes that get me in trouble."

"Yeah, you did say you fell in love with Samantha based on those orbs of hers."

"Please don't remind me that I ever used the L-word and that woman's name in the same sentence." Lincoln shivered as he rose. "Mind if I borrow your son? I want to go to the library."

"You don't need my child to do that. But yeah, I'm sure he'll be happy to go with you. However, as strange is this is going to sound, I don't want him there all day. That boy should be outside, throwing a ball around. Or chasing some girl."

"What a double standard you have."

"Try having kids and you might understand." Tal pulled out a key fob from his pocket. "It's not much, but you might as well use my old Jeep until you can manage to buy yourself a vehicle."

"Thanks, because my next question was, can I borrow—"

"Get out of here." Tal slapped Lincoln on the shoulder. "Let me know how I can help. Or anyone else from search and rescue. You already know Ethan, Rocky, and Brayden. But there's an entire group of men and woman, all with skills that might come in handy, at your fingertips."

"I'll keep that in mind." He turned and strolled through the house. Time to head to the library and make some small talk.

SINCE HER FATHER DIED, Stormi had entered Zero Gravity's computer system twenty times or so. She started off small and checked out what she'd call low-level threat areas—places where she'd most likely go undetected. There wasn't anything useful where she played—no client data, no proprietary information. She had been on a fact-finding mission.

It was all about learning the coding. Learning the system. Learning where back doors might be found.

In the beginning, all she had was her intuition. A little tickle in the back of her head that needled her mind. No way would her father cut corners to make a name for himself. He didn't give a shit about stuff like that. While he believed in space exploration, he cared more about safety, not money or name recognition.

Do it right.

Not fast.

That was always his motto.

It didn't matter if you were the last person to bring something to the table. What mattered was if you had the legs and the strength to maintain whatever you created. If you didn't have that, you had shit.

When Stormi first broke into the rocket ship data hallway inside their mainframe, she was able to unlock the filing cabinet that stored the proprietary information regarding the thrusters and engines—basically, what makes the rocket, or in this case, the spaceplane, lift off the ground. This had been what her father had been working on. He'd been testing the system when it essentially overheated, exploded, and killed her dad and five other people.

Only, that couldn't be what happened. Her father would beg the company to pull the plug if there had been any safety issues at all. Hell, he'd go to the media himself if he had to.

However, her instincts weren't enough, and she had to face one big fat reality. She didn't really know her father.

Unfortunately, her little game of leaking information forced Zero Gravity to bring in the big guns. She couldn't be entirely sure if that person came in the form of one sexy ex-military British man, but she didn't believe in coincidences.

During her last trip into the mainframe, she found that Zero Gravity's new team used her father's design, or at least it looked like her father's designs. That meant there was nothing wrong with them. So, what the hell had happened when the damn rocket went up in flames? But she'd been chased out before she could pull any of that data out with her, and now she had to take a step back.

At least for a few days.

However, she had stopped the launch and even though it pissed off the one person who was on her side, it was the only way to bring attention to the spaceplane. To bring in outsiders to examine it and either prove it was faulty or that it was her father's original work. That somehow it would help prove someone had sabotaged the last rocket.

That it wasn't her father.

She didn't need to speak to her father to understand the kind of man he was. He was a rule follower, and it's one of the many reasons he hated her job. He thought an ethical hacker was an oxymoron, and in many ways, it was. But without someone like her, people like her ex-husband would always come out on top.

Sadly, in the case of Zero Gravity, she might have fucked herself when it came to getting back in their system.

Now, she had to decide whether spending time with Lincoln was a good idea or whether she should continue playing the introverted librarian.

It wasn't that much of a stretch.

She glanced over her computer screen from behind the main counter at the public library and groaned. As if on cue, the man strolled through the doors with Tal's teenage son.

Game on.

She squared her shoulders, pushed her black-rimmed glasses up her nose, and smiled. "Good…" She lifted her wrist and glanced at her watch. "…afternoon." She waved her hand toward the far corner. "Suzie's finishing putting the returns away and prepping for the afternoon toddler reading group if you want to go help her, Chad."

"Sure." Chad nodded like a bobblehead before racing off.

"He's a good kid," she said.

"He told me this is your favorite." Lincoln set a to-go mug on the counter along with a paper bag. "His dad thinks he comes here because he has a crush on you. But could it be because he's got the hots for someone closer to his own age?"

She tilted her head. "You're kidding, right? Tal doesn't know about him and Suzie?"

"Not really." Lincoln chuckled. "How hot and heavy is this teenage romance?"

"I wouldn't describe it as any of those things. But they do like each other. A lot. How does Tal and Heather not know about this? Technically, only Suzie is on the volunteer list, but we don't mind Chad helping out. He's quite knowledgeable and he's good with kids."

Lincoln glanced over his shoulder and ran his fingers through his hair. "Not sure what to do with that juicy piece of intel. I don't want to toss the kid under the bus, but I'm sure his folks would like to know his real reason for being here all the time, especially when my buddy is a little worried about his lack of desire to do all the other things he enjoys this summer."

She raised her hands. "Not my place or my business, unless they do something inappropriate in this building and neither one has. Not yet anyway." She took the paper mug and lifted it. "Thank you for this. The coffee here sucks."

"You're welcome." He nodded. "Is there a private room I can use for a few hours? I have some research to do. I brought my own computer, so all I need is a table and little privacy. The house I rented won't be ready for me to move in for another few hours and my stuff isn't coming until six tonight anyway."

"Sure thing. Why don't you follow me." She snagged a set of keys from under the counter to room four. The one thing she hadn't been prepared for when she decided to move to Fallport was how utterly small it was and how everyone knew each other and their business. While Lake George could be considered a small town, it was spread out. She hadn't lived in the village. No, she grew up on Assembly Point and in the winter months, it was often isolating.

Probably one of the reasons she'd learned to love being alone.

Until her mother died and her father took the job with Zero Gravity, moving them to their offices in Maryland. She loved living on Chesapeake Bay, but she missed the Adirondacks. So much so, the only colleges she applied to were near that area.

Getting into MIT had been a dream come true.

Starting Fortress Technologies with her husband and moving to Saratoga Springs, which was closer to her childhood home, had been a dream come true.

That was until it all came crumbling down.

"You can have this room for the next four hours." She stuck the key inside the hole and pushed open the door. “The Wi-Fi code is on the table. Is there anything else I can help you with?”

“I do need to get a library card.” He winked.

“Hand over your driver’s license, and I’ll bring one back as soon as I can.”

“Thanks.” He took her hand, lifted it to his lips, and kissed it. “One more thing. Does the library have any books on the history of Zero Gravity? Specifically, their plans for spaceflight?”

Her heart jumped to her throat. Her skin prickled. “There are a slew of books on Zero Gravity. I can show you where they are located and you can pick out which ones tickle your fancy,” she said. “To be honest, that’s an area that I’m not overly familiar with. Technical things go right over my head. While I love all books, nonfiction included, anything that requires that kind of brain power gives me a headache.”

“Really? I’m fascinated by the concept of spaceflight. Have been since I thought the moon was made out of cheese.”

She laughed. “I wouldn’t be caught dead in a rocket ship. Not for the good of mankind and certainly not for the pure fun of it. I don’t even like to fly.”

“When I first joined the Special Boat Service, I wanted to be a pilot, but Tal had other plans for me and since he saved my life, I followed him like a sad pathetic puppy.” Lincoln chuckled. It was rich and deep and filled her stomach with butterflies. “I did eventually take lessons a few years ago. It’s amazing. Planes are incredible pieces of machinery. I've studied them much like I have computers. Now I'm doing that with rockets and shuttles. The idea that someday we all could be taking trips to space blows my mind." He raised his hand and made an explosion sign from the side of his temple, smiling like a big kid. His excitement was palpable. And genuine.

Perhaps he was just a geek who enjoyed all things technical.

She could relate to that.

"The books you're looking for are around the corner." She stepped outside the room and pointed down the hall. "Just go down there and take a left by the bathrooms. The books on Zero Gravity are on the second bookstack. If you can't find what you're looking for, I'll be at the main desk. Just come find me, and I'll do a search and see if we have something somewhere else in the library."

"Thanks, I really appreciate your help."

"Anytime." She smiled. "I better get back to my post." Turning, she double-timed it back through the library, hoping her body didn't tremble on the outside like it did on the inside.

Tonight, she would have to do a deep dive into Lincoln. She wasn't as concerned about his past. But she needed to find out more about what he was doing in Fallport. Specifically, what company he worked for and if he was working with Zero Gravity.

Hell, she had half a mind to hack into the library

Wi-Fi and watch what the man was doing. But if he was half as good as she was, he'd either bring his own secure line to do his work, or he'd lay a trap.

Fuck.

She needed to know one way or another.

CHAPTER FOUR

Growing up poor and on the streets had taught Lincoln about desperation. By the time he'd turned sixteen, he would have done almost anything for a little cash and food in his belly.

Patience wasn't part of that equation.

That came with time with Tal and time in the Royal Navy.

Now. years later, patience had become a natural state. His best friend. A way of life.

He leaned back in his chair and stared at his computer screens. It had taken him until nearly two in the morning to set up his home office precisely how he'd wanted it so his back wasn't to the door. That drove him batshit crazy in any situation.

The rest of his home was a complete disaster. The furniture had yet to be placed where he wanted it. The only thing he'd managed to assemble had been his bed, but that's because his body had demanded sleep.

His mind? Well, that had taken a good couple of shots of whiskey to get that sucker to calm down after yesterday.

Someone had hacked into the library's Wi-Fi, but that person made it appear as though they weren't trying to look at what he was doing, but to steal electronic books. How oddly interesting. Not only that, but it appeared they were in Southern California.

Damn, she was fucking good.

Because it had to be Stormi.

Who else could it be?

One of his computers rang with a secure call from Fool's Gold, Colorado.

Darius.

A few years ago, he worked with Darius and another Brotherhood Protectors agent, Wyatt Bixby, during an op involving two MI6 agents. While Lincoln did have an ego, it wasn't too big to admit that both Darius and Wyatt had mad skills when it came to hacking. They knew more than Lincoln, and he wasn't opposed to asking for help when he needed it.

Especially when he knew he could trust these men with his life.

Perhaps not quite like he could with Tal, but there was a lot of history there. And Tal didn't have the computer experience. Lincoln also wanted to keep Tal out of it as much as he could. At least for now. Lincoln needed more information about the players, especially if he was going to upset the balance in his best friend's life.

"Hey, Darius. How are you doing? How's Fenmore? How's the baby?"

"Not a baby anymore," Darius said. "And Fenmore's pregnant again."

"Congratulations. That's awesome."

"We're pretty happy about it. But this will be it for us. We're not getting any younger," Darius said. "I'm sure I don't have to ask, but I need to know how secure this line is."

"I followed your protocols."

"Thank you for that," Darius said. "Fenmore had to jump through some hoops to get this and it could put Stormi in danger. Not to mention, the FBI agent who handled her case, who got her in witness protection, is in the dark about a few things."

Lincoln leaned forward, snagging his mug of coffee, and he took a sip while he digested that intel. "Let's start with, why would Stormi be in danger? Her husband is in jail. It's believed he acted alone. It wasn't as if he fucked with the mob. He messed with corporate America and stole money. There weren't, and still aren't, any death threats, which begs the question. Why WITSEC for Stormi?"

"One of the things I was able to uncover—which was buried deep—is that two of the companies that laundered money, did so for some pretty nasty people.

The kind of people who use bullets to deal with shit, not words. So, yeah, her life could be in danger if anyone ever found out she was still alive and she was the one who blew the whistle."

"How did I miss that?" Lincoln asked softly.

After he'd found out Samantha was screwing around, Lincoln's life had turned upside down. He'd loved her. He'd wanted to marry her. Even have children with her, which was something he never thought he'd want. In an instant, she destroyed his soul and crushed his heart.

He spent a couple of months making love to a bottle of bourbon. He couldn't think straight, much less work. He made dozens of mistakes that cost their clients collectively over a million dollars. Frankly, he wasn't sure why Samantha kept him on, except maybe her own guilt.

But what killed him now was, Samantha had shaken his confidence. He questioned his abilities. If he even had any real skills to begin with.

"First, it wasn't reported on. The Feds, the cops, everyone kept that from the press. And for whatever reason, the assholes who were laundering their money through those companies never said anything either."

"Any idea why?"

"Yeah. They quickly found new businesses. Besides, it was in their best interest to keep their mouths quiet. Bringing attention to it would bring down a world of hurt on them and the focus on their bosses. Not a good idea," Darius said. "As far as why you didn't find it, well, that's because the FBI made it a side note. Fenmore told me they will do that if they don't even want their people to know the details behind the deal. It helps keep their charges safe."

"I suppose that makes sense, but don't they need to know all the facts? What if Stormi's cover is blown?"

"She has her handler, who knows all the sordid details. But our government can be secretive. It's both good and bad. Which brings me to the part that Kara is in the dark about," Darius said. "And I think you need a little history lesson on this FBI agent. You see, she started out in the Violent Crimes Division in DC. She worked a serial killer case with her detective husband, though he wasn't her husband at the time. That brought her to the Rochester, New York, office as the agent in charge."

"Why was she even on a case out of Saratoga? Wouldn't that fall under the Albany office?"

"It would. But the hack was for a company with headquarters in Rochester. She worked as part of a task force but ended up taking lead. She's well respected. Well-liked. And damn fucking smart. She never believed Stormi had anything to do with the hack and she went a little rogue to prove it. Caused a rift with some other agents. One in particular, whom my wife knows quite well and this is where it gets dicey. Special Agent James Hallenbeck, who worked an undercover case a few years back in your area with one of your search and rescue team members, also worked a case connected to Zero Gravity."

"I don't like the sound of this."

"It gets better," Darius said.

"What Kara doesn't know, and now will probably need to be read in on, is Stormi's father, while not officially in WITSEC, does have the protection of one federal agent."

"What the fuck." Lincoln sloshed his coffee down the front of his shirt. "Are you telling me that Dante Norris isn't dead?"

"Nope. Talk about a clusterfuck of epic proportions."

"Does this other agent know that Stormi is alive?"

"Yes. While Kara pissed him off when she went rogue, they have communicated a few times over the last year. However, Jimmy is keeping Kara at a safe distance, and Kara most likely isn't telling Jimmy about what Stormi is up to," Darius said. "This is what happens when the left hand doesn't speak to the right hand."

Lincoln rubbed his temples. "Stormi went into witness protection three years ago. I can see how she might get lost in the shuffle. There was no trial. Her husband pleaded guilty to a slightly lesser charge. But I would think the Feds might want to use her skills on this one."

"Jimmy doesn't want her anywhere near it because he doesn't want her knowing about her dad. Too risky in general and I agree with that assessment," Darius said. "Are you sure it's her you saw inside their system?"

"I can't be one hundred percent positive at this point." He tapped his fingers on the keyboard, pulling up his files on Dante. "According to all my information, she and her dad stopped communicating regularly after she married. Outside of a few emails or text messages on holidays or birthdays, they might as well have been strangers. But it makes me wonder if maybe she knows he's alive and is doing his bidding."

"Anything is possible, but you should know Jimmy is quite computer-savvy," Darius said. "Which leaves you with quite the conundrum."

"Wonderful." Lincoln chuckled. "Zero Gravity is sketchy as hell. I've been going down this rabbit hole that's not what I was hired to do. I mean, I already patched their security breach. I am working on finding the person, and I should be writing code to make sure it never happens again. But I find myself wanting to make a trap for whoever the hacker is, follow them into the system, and watch them search for whatever it is they want. It would certainly give me insight on what their goals are. And if Zero Gravity is on the up-and-up. Or if they are cutting corners, like the leaks suggest. And the worst part is I don't want to let my boss or Zero Gravity in on what I'm doing."

"Look, Fenmore is reaching out to Jimmy today. He's a good man. Once they chat, hopefully, he'll be willing to talk to you. That might give you some insight on what you should do next."

"Don't have her go too far out on a limb for me. I've got enough information that I can—"

"Don't go hacking into the FBI databases. I've done that before and it's never a good thing. Nearly cost me my job."

"Are you seriously telling me you got caught?"

"I'm telling you that you will." Darius laughed. "Wait for either Fenmore to call you, or Jimmy. While she doesn't know Kara, she knows people who do. She'll find a way to have a conversation with her as well and maybe, just maybe, Kara will reach out to you."

"I can be patient."

"One more thing," Darius said. "Jimmy has a bigger tie to Fallport you should know about. His brother-in-law is Brayden Gibson."

"I know Brayden. He and his wife came to the UK for their honeymoon," Lincoln said. "I guess I'm tossing the no dating rule out the fucking window."

"Sweet Jesus. Not a good idea and not just because getting involved with the object of an investigation is a recipe for disaster," Darius said. "But you're still working for your ex and that's—"

"I can handle Samantha. And I'm not actually going to get involved with Stormi. Just take her out. Get her to trust me, and hopefully, she'll slip up and give me something I can use. If she's the one hacking into Zero

Gravity, I want to know why. Maybe she knows something I don't. I need to cover my bases."

"Right. I've seen her picture. Her eyes. You can tell yourself that all you want. Just be careful, man."

"I'll talk with you soon." He ended the call. "Jesus, that was a lot to take in," he mumbled. It totally changed the direction of his research and how he was going to handle his job moving forward.

He glanced at his watch. He had a Zoom meeting with Samantha and David Caulkin in forty minutes. He was going to have to stall. That he could handle.

Reaching for his cell, he pulled up Stormi's contact information. Time to turn up the British charm. He tapped her number. It rang three times before she answered.

"Hello?"

"Hey, Stormi. It's Lincoln. How are you today?"

"Just fine, and you?"

"Trying to get settled into my house, which is never fun." He chuckled. "I was wondering if you had plans for dinner tonight?"

"I thought you didn't know me well enough to ask me out on a date."

"Ouch. That hurt," he said. "And it doesn't have to be a date. Not in the traditional sense of the word. I haven't had the chance to do any major grocery shopping yet and I'm really not in the mood to do it today, much less cook. Nor do I want to eat alone or order takeout because I'll only sit and stare at my computer screens and work. I can't call Tal, because his son is a little pissed at me for informing his parents of his budding romance with Suzie."

"Oh, that was not cool."

"Chad and Suzie left me with no choice when I caught them making out behind the library."

"Come on. You were a teenager once. You could have played the blind man," she said.

"I suppose, only I wasn't the only one who was there. Suzie's mom had been looking for them too. While she doesn't have a problem with the kids hanging out, she doesn't want them hiding their budding relationship or playing kissy-face all the time at their age. Neither does Tal and Heather. It was for the best. Besides, it evens the playing field with Marisa and her boyfriend."

"I'm not sure I see how, but it's not my business and as long as Suzie can continue to volunteer, I'm not sure I care."

"And this has nothing to do with where we should go to dinner tonight."

"I never agreed to that," Stormi said. "But I do have to eat and all I have is the makings for a salad. How about we meet at On The Rocks. I've never been there but I know they make a mean cheeseburger and tater tots."

"Isn't that the bar that Zeke Calhoun owns?"

"I believe the owner's name is Zeke, but to be honest, I've only ordered takeout. I know the food is good. I can't speak for the atmosphere. However, Tal and Heather go there every once in a while, and the girls from the book club at the library are always raving about it."

"On The Rocks it is," he said. "I can swing by and pick you up, if that would be easier."

"Nah. That might feel like too much of a date and I wouldn't want to give you the wrong impression."

"It might be too late for that." His fingers hovered over his keyboard. "I'll see you at six." He ended the call and tapped on an encrypted email from one Special Agent James Hallenbeck. It took three minutes to unravel the layers to get at the actual message.

Lincoln found himself a little smitten with Jimmy considering all that the message contained was a date, time, address, and one sentence.

Don't be late and don't tell anyone you're meeting me.

"Trust me, I won't." He filed the message in a folder on his computer with the rest of the information pertaining to Stormi. Separate from his work files for Zero Gravity. He had to compartmentalize the two. At least for now. Even though the two were so intertwined it was insane.

He stood, ripping off his shirt, and made a beeline for the laundry room. He treated the coffee stains and found a clean button-down shirt. One that might be worthy of a date and one that didn't need ironing. His least favorite chore. As if he had one he enjoyed doing.

As soon as he returned to his office, his phone buzzed.

His boss. Or his ex. Depending on how one looked it at. Right now, he didn't care to ponder either.

"Samantha." He rolled his chair in front of his main computer and pulled up the latest information he had on the security breach. "You're early for this call." Which pissed him off for a variety of reasons. He had so many questions for Samantha, but he wasn't sure he was prepared to ask a single one.

Mostly because if she was up to her eyeballs in this shit, she'd lie.

"I want a heads-up on where we stand and why you haven't implemented any new software to their system. You've barely even made a patch to the breach." Samantha had gotten her start at NCSC or the National Cyber Security Centre. She spent eight long years with that department. She told Lincoln it was so boring it reduced her to tears. When they met, she'd been working as an ethical hacker for a different company and was itching to start her own firm.

Enter Lincoln and what few dollars he had saved.

"Besides the fact I literally just landed Stateside yesterday, I've barely had a chance to get my office set up, which means I haven't been able to write the necessary code to close the holes," he said. "And even then, I'm not sure that will solve their problem." Holding her off was going to be a difficult dance.

"That makes no sense. You're one of the best in the business. You can make anything nearly unhackable."

"I find it interesting that you, of all people, are complimenting me," he said. "I mean, two months ago, you called me a washed-up asshole."

"Because you were acting like a dick."

"I wonder what could have caused that," he mumbled.

"I don't want to fight with you. We have a job to do and there's no reason this can't be buttoned up nice and neat in a few weeks. Without that breach handled, they don't feel comfortable launching."

He found it fascinating that she was pushing him so hard when, before he got on that plane, she wanted things done right, not fast. "But David was sure it was an inside job. He's yet to give me names. Without anyone to target, I'm going down a black hole of every employee. That makes this part of the job that much harder. I'm looking at keystrokes of at least fifty people over the course of three months. Now why the hell would he want to launch if he's worried one of his own is sabotaging his company?"

"That's not our problem. We're not cops. And you're not in the Royal Navy anymore. We were hired to do one job. So, let's do it."

He pinched the bridge of his nose. When he first started working with Samantha, this was the part of the job he liked. In some ways, it reminded him of the Special Boat Service. Get in, take care of the target, don't ask questions, and get out. Granted, the older he got, the more he wanted to know all the whys.

This was the kind of case that demanded answers.

Lives could be at stake and he couldn't let it go.

Especially not now.

Time to take a calculated risk.

"Something doesn't feel right."

"You and your damn gut instincts," Samantha said under her breath. "It's a security system. One they need. One we were hired to provide."

"No. They wanted us to do a little more than that, like find the culprit. Right? Isn't that why I'm the guy doing this job?"

"If you could, yes. But not if it means delaying this launch any more, or leaving them open to another hack, which is what you're doing. I knew you'd want a little time to look at their system. I gave it to you. But now is the time to do what the client wants."

"I have a suggestion," he said.

"Oh, this should be good."

"Since the launch and testing is postponed until after this inquiry, we have a little more time to play with things. I will go ahead and set up a new system. I'll monitor, both from the inside and the outside. But I only want me doing that. No one else, including you. That will give us total integrity of the output. But I want to do it in phases. One that will require opening Zero Gravity up a little."

“Are you talking about setting up a trap for our hacker?” Samantha asked.

He was surprised she didn’t comment on the fact he wanted her staying the fuck out of his work.

“Something like that.”

“What if they don’t come back?”

“Come on, Samantha. Tell me if it were you and you were leaking that kind of information out to the press, would you stay away?”

“Interesting point,” Samantha said. “But you’re not keeping me in the dark. It’s my ass on the line. I want to be able to see what you’re doing.”

“Nope. We do this my way, or—”

“Or what? You walk? Because you can’t do that. I either own your ass for another two years, or you finish this job.”

He leaned back and folded his arms. “You have two choices, Samantha. I can upload a new system. A good one. The best. But if someone close to David has been fucking around inside the digital data halls, even I won’t be able to stop them, unless I can sit back and watch, without you or anyone else monitoring. It’s your choice.”

“Are you suggesting that we say the job is done, but then spy on them?”

“Kind of,” he said. “We do it in stages. Starting with a patch, which I can do shortly. But I need you to trust me.”

"That requires you to do the same of me. Can you do that?" she asked.

"I'm going to have to," he said without any conviction. But he'd also make sure he'd be able to see anyone coming inside his new system, including her.

Especially her.

"I never meant to hurt you."

He burst out laughing. It wasn't an appropriate response, but hell, he caught her screwing another man—one he called friend—on his damn desk. Didn't she think that would tear his heart out?

"Honestly, I didn't," she said softly. Her voice trembled and it sounded almost as if she meant it.

Only, Samantha didn't have true feelings. The only things she cared about were money, success, and… hell, he had no idea.

"You have a funny way of showing that," he said. "I need you to stay out of the system while I'm working on this job and I want to know why Zero Gravity is so important to you."

"They aren't," Samantha said a little too quickly.

"Seriously? Did you really believe I wouldn't know immediately that you wrote their initial security system?" Nothing like showing his hand, but he figured it was the only way to get her to agree to back off.

"I wasn't the only coder on that assignment and it was right before I started CyberGuard Solutions."

"Are you telling me that they don't know you had anything to do with the original system?"

"Something like that."

"Shit, Samantha. David might not be too thrilled with that juicy piece of intel," Lincoln said. "Not that I'm going to say anything, because I want the fuck out of this insanity. But it's all the more reason to let me figure this out and for you to go get your nails done."

"I'll give you space, but you've got three weeks to make sure Zero Gravity has their new system loaded and running."

"Got it."

"Have fun with the client. I'm going to ditch out on you."

"Why am I not surprised," he mumbled.

"Send me a report." The line went dead.

He leaned back and rubbed his neck. Samantha was like every other high-caliber computer geek who had worked for the government. While she was always willing to bend the rules when it came to getting information, she wasn't so willing to do so when giving it. She followed strict protocols when writing security code. Her system was second to none, and her hacking skills were scary.

When Samantha first started her company, she wanted to protect organizations and people from the darkness that lurked on the dark web.

Or so she said.

However, he was so busy with his deployments that he didn't see the kinds of jobs she took, and honestly, he didn't pay attention—not until he started working for her himself. The difference between him and everyone else was that he was an independent contractor with a term contract and not an employee. It was a technicality that he demanded.

She hadn't really been on board with that idea at first, but since he'd invested a lot of money, that's how he wanted it. He also wanted to be able to do other things, like possibly take jobs that utilized his other skills, which meant he couldn't afford to punch a time clock. Being a contract employee meant he got paid per job and didn't have to worry about showing up for work every day. He'd believed it was a win-win. Little did he know, he was giving his fiancée permission to continue cheating.

He pushed all those thoughts to the side. Time to talk David off the ledge. Then he was off to meet a sexy lady and try not to flirt too hard, or worse, take her to bed, because that thought kept popping into his head like a recurring dream that just wouldn't go away.

CHAPTER FIVE

Stormi pulled back the main doors to On The Rocks and strolled inside. It smelled like fresh roasted peanuts mixed with whiskey and sizzling meat on the grill.

Her stomach immediately growled, which was better than twisting up in a knot like it had been five minutes ago. Her aversion to people had lessened some since she'd come to Fallport and had been working in the library. But socializing with them, well, that she could still do without.

For the last three years, she'd kept more to herself than she ever had, and that wasn't hard to do.

She followed the hostess to a table on the side of the bar and checked her watch, wishing she'd been late, instead of ten minutes early.

"Pam will be your waitress, but can I start you off with a beverage?" the hostess asked.

"A tequila on the rocks with a lime."

"Pam will bring that right over."

Stormi pulled out her cell. Lincoln wasn't an easy man to find information on. Not surprising, considering he'd spent most of his life with the British Armed Forces.

Everything he'd told her about his past—about his parents dying and living in foster care—had been true. She'd learned he retired a year ago, but she had no idea the circumstances, and she wasn't about to hack into the British government—not today, anyway.

Outside of that, the only interesting thing she'd found was that he lived with a woman for three years and was engaged until about six months ago.

And she owned a cybersecurity firm called Cyber-Guard Solutions.

Lincoln wasn't listed as an employee or an investor. He wasn't listed anywhere on the website and Stormi wasn't about to use her skills to go find out how he was linked to it, because she knew for damn sure he was.

But she couldn't have a digital footprint linked back to her and knew it eventually would be.

Especially if he was here to find and fix the security breach in Zero Gravity.

She should pay her bill and leave this bar before he showed up, but before that thought could go any further, the gorgeous Brit strolled into On The Rocks with a wicked smile and his damn sexy swagger.

He was a tall drink of danger wrapped in a sweet

and salty pastry that no one in their right mind could resist.

He paused at a table in the center of the room, giving Brayden Gibson, a member of the local search and rescue team, a manly hug. Also at the table was Weston Campbell and Blaze Wright, also part of search and rescue. A minute later, Zeke came from behind the bar and shook Lincoln's hand while the waitress set her drink down in front of her.

"Thank you," Stormi said.

"You look familiar." The waitress narrowed her eyes.

"I work at the library," Stormi offered as she swallowed her fear, wondering if perhaps Pam recognized her from her past life. Pam didn't look familiar, but that didn't mean anything.

"Can't say that I've ever been inside a bookstore, much less a library." Pam continued to squint. "I'm new to town, so I don't know many people. Are you from the area?"

"No," Stormi admitted. "Where are you from?"

"Upstate New York."

Fuck. Fuck. Fuck. "Well, I'm from Maryland. Grew up on the Chesapeake. Can't say that I've ever been to the great state of New York," Stormi said, hoping that nipped whatever this girl thought she recognized in Stormi.

"You're not missing much, that's for sure. I was happy to get out."

"What brought you to Fallport?" Stormi asked, telling herself that knowledge was power. She also hoped to get the girl's last name so she could dig into her past.

"Sadly, I moved here about a year ago with my boyfriend who dumped me six months ago." Pam shrugged. "I have no desire to go home with my tail between my legs."

"Can't say as I blame you."

Pam glanced over her shoulder. "Who's the sexy new guy?" She planted her hand on her hip and gave Lincoln the once-over. "I know all the search and rescue team members and he's not one of them, though he's awful dreamy."

"That's Lincoln. He's friends with Tal and from the UK."

"Oh, yeah. I've heard Tal had a friend who was moving here." The waitress turned her attention back to Stormi. "Can I get you something else?"

"Not this second." She pointed toward Lincoln, as if to mark her territory. "I'm waiting on him."

"Oh really." The waitress cocked a brow. "Is it a date? Or can I ask for his number?"

Stormi should tell the cute little blonde that this wasn't a date and she could prance her boobs all up in Lincoln's face if she wanted to, but a sudden burst of unwanted jealousy bellowed through her veins like a raging wildfire. "That wouldn't be advisable," Stormi said, lifting her hand. She wiggled her fingers, waving to Lincoln.

He smiled, nodding his head.

"Do you know what he'd like to drink?" Pam asked as she shifted her weight, nudging out her other hip.

"He'll take one of these." She pointed to her glass. If he didn't like it, she'd drink it, but she wasn't about to admit to Pam that she had no idea what her date enjoyed.

"Coming right up." Pam turned on her heel and marched off as if she were running from that same fire that had erupted inside Stormi's body.

Damn. Stormi wasn't normally the kind of girl who got her panties in a twist over a man. Not even when she suspected Kurt had been cheating. What did affect her was when he fucked with their business. That cut her to the bone.

Though, seeing the pictures of his indiscretions had made it easier to send that asshole to prison.

But the bigger issue that she should be dealing with, and would be as soon she got home and in front of her computer, was, could Pam possibly know who she was or could she figure it out?

"Hey there." Lincoln slipped into the booth across from her and smiled. "You look pretty."

"If I wasn't wearing jeans and a basic T-shirt, I'd simply say thank you."

He cocked his head. "And a woman can't look nice in that outfit?"

"I suppose." She shrugged.

Pam appeared with his drink. "Your date ordered you this." She set it down in front of him, leaning over, letting her breasts dangle in his face a little too long. "I hope you like tequila."

"Now why would my date order me something I wouldn't appreciate." He lifted his glass to his lips and sipped. "That's perfect, babe. You know me so well."

Stormi rolled her eyes.

"Can I get you folks an appetizer? Or are you ready to order?" Pam asked.

"Shall I?" Lincoln winked.

"By all means, *honey.*"

"We'll have an order of medium wings to share. Then the lady will have the cheeseburger and tater tots, and I'll do the same, but I want onion rings. Both burgers we want medium rare," he said.

"Coming right up." Pam stuffed her pad and pencil back in her apron and strolled off toward the kitchen.

"Looks like you made a new best friend." He took another gulp of his drink.

"Sorry," she mumbled. "But to add a little context to that, she all but wanted to know if she could have your number."

Lincoln laughed. "My boys over there were just giving me a little heads-up on Pam, the desperate waitress, in hot pursuit of a husband. I'm told she moved to town a year ago, got her heart broken, and has been on the hunt ever since." Lincoln leaned closer. "Blaze mentioned she has a type. And that's anyone who wears or wore a uniform. That shit makes me crazy."

"I imagine it would, but you could have her for dessert if you wanted."

"Not interested."

"You don't find her attractive?" Stormi leaned back and studied his facial expressions, which always seemed to be in playful mode. He had to be one of the most laid-back men she'd ever met. Even when he was knee-deep in research at the library. She shouldn't find that utterly fascinating, but she did.

"That's a relative term."

"What do you mean?" This was not the conversation she was itching to have with Lincoln. Only, she had no idea how to segue from this topic to his work.

"At face value, taking no context at all, she's drop-dead gorgeous. But once you learn her backstory, what her goals and motivations in life are, beauty means jack shit. It can actually make a person ugly as hell." He lifted his lime and squeezed it into his drink.

"You're judging a woman based on what others have said about her."

"Perhaps a little. But she did shove her boobs in my face." He shivered. "That is not the way to get me to notice you. As a matter of fact, it's the perfect way to turn me off," he said. "But why are we sitting here chatting about our server for the evening." He rested his arms on the table and leaned forward. "I'd rather be getting to know you better."

"You certainly are a charmer."

"I don't know about that. My ex would tell you that I couldn't sweet-talk my way into trouble, much less out of it. She'd also call me the biggest asshole on the planet."

"I think all exes have tainted views of their past relationships."

"You're probably right there." He smiled as Pam, the flirty-pants waitress placed the chicken wings and two plates on the table, along with two fresh drinks. "Zeke said these and the first round are on him." She smiled, staring at Lincoln, her back to Stormi. "I just want to say, thank you for your service. I'm sure you'll make a great addition to the Fallport Search and Rescue team."

"Thank you." Lincoln piled a few wings on a plate and placed them in front of Stormi, keeping his gaze fixated on her and nowhere else.

If this were a real date, this man would have her hook, line, and sinker. Hell, she wouldn't kick him out of bed, that was for damn sure. Hopefully, she wouldn't find herself in a predicament where she had to actually say no, because that might be impossible, considering it had been over a year since she'd had sex with anything other than hard, cold plastic.

"Babe, is there anything else you need?" He placed his hand over hers and ran his thumb over the inside of her wrist.

Her skin tingled under his touch. "I'm good."

"Your dinner will be up in about twenty." Pam scurried off.

"How is it that you can be mean, without actually being mean?"

"I don't want to hurt the girl's feelings, but I did want to make two, maybe three points clear." He tapped his finger on the table. "The first one is that I'm not interested in her, at all. The second one is I'm sitting in this booth with you and that's where my attention will lie." He took a wing and gobbled up half of it.

"And what's the third?" She waited patiently for him to finish chewing while she tried desperately not to stare at his sweet, delectable lips.

"While you've made it perfectly clear this isn't a date, I wouldn't mind changing your mind about that."

She arched a brow as she nibbled on her food, contemplating how to respond, while her heart hammered wildly in her chest. Dating him was out of the question. Pumping him for information, that was a different story. But how did she do that?

Glancing up over her wing, she swallowed as he reached across the table, took her hand, and sucked on her fucking finger.

Why the fuck did he have to order this appetizer?

"Sorry. I couldn't resist the temptation."

"Try to," she managed.

His right eye twitched. "I can't tell if you're mad and trying to find a way to turn me down nicely, or if you're considering letting the flirting continue because you're enjoying it."

"What I'm enjoying is this wing. I lived in New York and it's hard to find good Buffalo style wings. This is pretty damn close." She tossed her bone on the plate and snagged another one.

"Ah. You're an avoider."

"My ex-husband called me that all the time." She shrugged. "Perhaps he was right."

"You were married?"

"Does that bother you?" She resented how much damn fun she was having and if his lips landed on hers, she'd suck on his tongue. Those kinds of thoughts she needed to banish from her mind.

"No. But I guess I'm a little surprised since you're so young. How long were you married and when did you get divorced?"

"I got married at twenty-five and divorced by twenty-seven." So much of her fake history was blended in with reality. This was a little too close to her real life and she hated talking about it, but it seemed necessary.

"Do you mind if I ask what happened?"

She wiped her fingers on a napkin and pushed her plate aside. "We were young and stupid. Didn't know each other long enough or well enough. He was all about being social and going out with friends and I would much rather stay at home with a book or a movie. At first, our differences seemed cute. We joked about how opposites attract and I'd make an effort with his friends, and he'd stay home. But that only lasted about a year. He wanted to have parties every weekend. Or have me cook for his poker buddies. And the trips." She waved her hand dramatically over her plate. "I hated going on vacation with his snotty friends and their stuck-up wives. We started fighting all the time. He'd go out. I'd stay home. One day, he told me he was in love with someone else and I told him not to let the door hit him on the way out." Damn. She had no idea she could lie that well. However, the emotion behind the words wasn't phony.

"That was three years ago. Have you dated anyone special since?"

She shook her head. That was at least the truth. "Your turn. You keep mentioning an ex. Tell me about her. I take it she's who Heather fixed you up with."

"Good deduction skills," he said. "Unfortunately, I'm still tied to Samantha for a little while."

"How so?"

"I do contract work for the company she owns. To make a very long story short, I have one last job to do for her, and then I'm in the clear. That can't happen fast enough for my liking."

"Why'd you break up?"

"A plethora of reasons, but the main one was she cheated on me with someone we both worked with. That's a deal-breaker for me."

"Probably for most people." She polished off her

first drink and brought her second one closer, though she'd sip it for the rest of the evening. The last thing she needed was to get drunk. "I'm sorry that happened to you."

"Better that I found out before we got married."

"You were engaged?" she asked as if she hadn't learned that from diving into his boss' social media posts. She found it odd that a cybersecurity person would have that kind of digital imprint. Of course, it wasn't a big one and it was used more for marketing than anything else.

"Not for very long, but I did spend five years with Samantha. It wasn't all bad. Just the last year. However, I suspect she was sleeping around with other men while I was deployed, so there's that."

"Not cool."

"Nope. It's not. But it's over and not something I like to dwell on." He tilted his head and narrowed one eye. "Tell me something. Aren't you at all concerned about your job as a librarian with the advent of the digital age? I mean ebooks are all the rage. And how many people, outside of old relics like me or parents who want to bring their kids to story hour, actually go to the library anymore?"

"Lots of people. My job is still useful and I'm learning every day about new technology." She plastered on her best smile. "We have digital libraries that require a library card. I have to help people with that. And book clubs use the library all the time. Not to mention that college and high school libraries are still in big demand. I could always go work there if I had to. Adapt or die, as they say."

"That's an excellent attitude, but libraries will become virtual. I can see in the near future that consumers won't even have to leave their homes to check out a book." He held up his hand. "Not that I would be for that, because I love the feel of a book in my hands, and I get drunk on the smell of the library."

"I know, right. It's intoxicating." Almost as much as the way a keyboard felt on her fingertips. "However, ebooks haven't completely taken over the marketplace."

"Oh, but they will. Just like cell phones have replaced landlines and streaming is killing cable."

"Next thing you're going to tell me is that AI (Artificial Intelligence) voices will take over for audiobook narrators."

He laughed. "Already happening. I listened to three last month. The voices were pretty good too."

"Now that just breaks my heart." She fanned herself. Only, all it did was make her pulse soar. She loved the idea of AI. It fascinated her on so many levels. And it was all around them. Some of the most basic daily functions today used some form of AI, even if people weren't aware they were engaging with it. But humans would do so many destructive things with AI. They always did. Not because AI was inherently bad. But because people were inherently greedy and had an insatiable thirst for power. "What about you? Aren't you worried that AI will take over your job? Replace what you do?" She raised her hand and coiled her fingers through her hair, tilting her head ever so slightly. "And what is that exactly, because I surely don't understand."

"The interesting thing about what I do in the private sector is that I'm the reason we need people like me." He winked.

"I'm not sure I follow." Only she knew exactly what he meant.

"It's simple and frankly, a problem as old as time." He smiled as if he'd unlocked the key to the human race. "Man created weapons. Humans have stated over time that their purpose was to defend. Or perhaps to survive. But in that quest to protect ourselves from the big bad wolf, we continue to use technology as a measuring stick of growth. Of our evolvement. However, all these big so-called advancements come with a big price. Going back to my weapons analogy, what started as a way to hunt food and protect our homes has turned into a way to destroy the world." He tapped his cell. "The things I can do behind technology are pretty scary. Used for the right reasons, they keep your data and our world safe. But when is enough enough? We've passed that line with weapons probably even before the nuclear bomb was built and used. And yet, we're still developing weapons of mass destruction. Technology could be a worse weapon because it holds the power to turn us against each other in different ways. I'd like to believe I'm part of the solution. Only, the fact that I exist kind of makes me part of the problem." He lifted his drink and downed it like a shot.

"I didn't understand a word you just said and now I have a headache." She rubbed her temple as Pam placed their dinners in front of them. It was a lame attempt to pretend his words confused her, when in reality, they excited her.

"Can I refill your drinks?" Pam asked.

"I'll have one more." Lincoln nodded. "Stormi? Would you like another?"

"I really shouldn't, but after that jumbled monologue of stuff I didn't understand, I could use one." Stormi smiled, lifted her drink, tipped back her head, and pounded the last few gulps. She shouldn't have, but it was the only way she'd get through the rest of the night, and she wasn't quite ready to call it quits.

"Coming right up." Pam turned and swayed her hips while she glanced over her shoulder.

Stormi had met a dozen men and women like Lincoln over the years, all wishing to get out of the game, all knowing they were trapped by the lines of code that called to them in their sleep.

It was as strong as any drug.

And just as powerful as money.

People like him wanted to make a difference in the world. They wanted to protect the innocent. Prevent the world from going to shit because of the advances that on the one hand made them feel safe, but on the other made them weak and vulnerable.

It was the ultimate paradox.

A matrix.

Technology was the very thing that brought about an easier way of life. Yet, it was destined to be mankind's destruction.

That was if you believed the techie philosophers of the world.

Sometimes she did, other times she didn't.

"Sorry about that." He plopped an onion ring into his mouth. "Looks like I've let my current case creep its way into our date."

"How so?" She sliced her burger into two halves. The longer she kept him on this topic, the better. While she was ninety percent sure Lincoln was the man poking around the digital halls of Zero Gravity, she wanted to be proof positive.

"I don't want to bore you, much less make your head hurt worse."

She batted her lashes and smiled as sweetly as she could. "I really am fascinated. It's just for a computer geek, you're a little more philosophical than I anticipated."

"Tal says my biggest problem is that I analyze everything like I'm a combination computer chip and detective." Lincoln chuckled. "Thing is, I don't trust my ex and she lied to me about this job." Lincoln held up his finger. "That's problem number one, but if I believe what she told me about it after I confronted her, it's not that big of a deal. Problem number two is that I stumbled onto something that I know I wasn't supposed to and I'm not sure if my ex knows anything about it. If she does, this is one fucked-up game, and I don't like where it's headed. And my final problem is I have no idea how to play the shitty hand I've been dealt."

"You've literally told me nothing and it sounds like a bad spy movie." She lowered her chin, licking her lips. "Does this have anything to do with Zero Gravity?" She held up her hand. "I only ask because of all the time you spent in the library researching them."

"I can't confirm or deny."

She clasped her hands and placed them on the table. "What can I do to help?"

"Nothing." He let out a long breath before raising his drink.

"Come on. I might not know much about computers, but I have a world of information at my fingertips. There's got to be something I can do to help you figure out what card to play." She cocked her head and swallowed her pulsating heart. This had to be the dumbest idea she'd ever had. Besides having no proof that Lincoln was indeed the hacker she'd seen in the digital hallways, even if he was the one, he'd been hired by Zero Gravity.

"Besides, if it has anything to do with Zero Gravity

and their launch, I wouldn't mind seeing them grounded for life."

"And why is that?" He held her stare with an unwavering gaze.

This was not how she planned on playing this, but currently, the old idea of keeping your enemies close kept tickling her brain. Only, was Lincoln the enemy? "I might have only met Marisa's boyfriend once, but he seems like a nice kid," Stormi said. "Between that, and watching you do all that research, I decided to check out the company, and I read the articles about the explosion last year. I also read the leaked content. Sounds like something weird is going on. I can help you, at least with the research part. I'm good at that." That last part was a calculated risk, but one she believed was worth taking. She needed to find out what the hell Lincoln was up to, why, and how she could use it to help not only shut down Zero Gravity, but save her father's reputation.

"I honestly can't comment on any of that and I'm sorry, but I can't use your help." He took her hand. "I do appreciate your wanting to." He pressed his lips against her skin. "It's getting late and I've got early conference calls. Tal told me you lived in town and that you could have walked here. Did you?"

She nodded.

"Well, then I best escort you to your front door." He waved to Pam, who scurried over, only to frown when he asked for the check, which he paid for in cash. "It's a nice evening and I could use some fresh air."

Stunned, she took the hand he offered. She needed a moment to collect her thoughts. No way would she let him blow her off like this. She'd let him walk her home and she'd do her best to offer support. A lending ear. Hell, she'd even suggest a second date. Anything to learn more about what he was doing. He spoke way too cryptically and she had to know what the hell was going on.

Her father's legacy was too important.

CHAPTER SIX

Lincoln entwined his fingers through Stormi's as he led her down the streets of Fallport in the direction of her rented home just on the outskirts of town. Her eagerness would be considered cute had it not been calculated. It had taken him hours to follow the digital trail of the library hack. He'd been impressed at the lengths she'd gone through to keep the hack from being traced. And had he not been one of the elites in his field, he would have missed several diversion tactics she used.

However, Lincoln knew without a shadow of a doubt she'd spied on him that first day in the library.

Add in the fact she was in WITSEC, something he had to protect at all costs.

He paused at the end of her driveway, resting his hands on her hips. "I'm sorry I'm being cagey about my job. Between the client wanting secrecy and my ex-fiancée making my life a living hell, I've ruined our first date. How can I make it up to you?"

She palmed his face. "You didn't ruin anything. Surprisingly, I had a really good time tonight."

"I'm not sure if I should be insulted or not." He kissed the inside of her palm. His heart beat a little faster while his stomach churned like sour milk. He wondered if he'd ever meet a woman who wouldn't betray his trust.

He sure as shit couldn't trust Samantha. Not when they were dating, and certainly not now. Although, he wasn't sure what, if anything, Samantha knew about Zero Gravity and the woman currently in his arms. Samantha was a lot of things, and he suspected this had more to do with saving face, considering she'd written most of the code that failed during the first breach to begin with when she'd worked for a different company.

That was motivation enough for Samantha.

But Stormi was an entirely different problem.

"You should be flattered and offended." She laughed. "I honestly thought that while I might find you charming, you'd also come across as pigheaded and arrogant. You did neither. I enjoyed myself tonight. I can't say I've had a good time with a man since my divorce."

"I swore off relationships after Samantha." He took her chin with his thumb and forefinger. This game. This dance. The whole entire fucking thing was too easy. He resented the betrayal of his own emotions.

The ones that made it so effortless to lean in and brush his mouth over her plump lips in a sweet and tender kiss.

God, she tasted like cotton candy. His tongue wrapped around hers in a deadly tango. To his soul and body, this was as real as it could possibly be.

But to the rest of him, it was about as fake as a set of eyelashes on a performer.

"I take it you're willing to go out with me again?" he asked.

"Against my better judgment, yes."

He pressed his hand against the small of her back and led her up the walkway. Someone should shoot him for the thoughts circling his brain like a vulture. "How about tomorrow night?"

Turning, she tapped her fingers against the keypad, unlocking the front door. "I've got a nice bottle of tequila. Would you like a nightcap?"

"Coming in might be against my better judgment," he whispered. He'd made numerous mistakes over his lifetime. Most of the big ones had been before he turned eighteen.

Or had to do with women.

Spending time with Stormi was one thing. He genuinely enjoyed her personality. She was smart. Witty. Fun. There wasn't anything he could find that he didn't like.

Except she was lying to him.

Only that wasn't entirely her fault. The government

had a hand in her lies. She honestly didn't have a choice. She needed to do it in order to survive. It had become her new normal. A way of life.

At least her new identity had, something he totally understood.

However, her sneaking around Zero Gravity was a different kind of lie. One that—depending on her goals and motivations—made her lies and betrayals quite different.

It also proposed an ethical dilemma for Lincoln.

It was one thing to use her by chatting her up. To learn information about what she did, or didn't know, simply by asking her questions.

It was quite another to take her to bed.

And he didn't have a logical reason for doing so, except he wanted to.

"It's just one drink." She tugged at his shirt, pulling him across the threshold. "I don't bite."

"Not the point."

"And what is the point, then?" she quizzed, her eyes narrowing slightly. The orange glow of the porch light cast an ethereal shimmer across her face. She was a dangerous woman. One he shouldn't even consider, and not just because of what he'd uncovered about her past.

Or even that he knew without a shadow of a doubt that she'd hacked into Zero Gravity.

He could almost live with those things, considering who she was.

But his heart was half-dead. It wouldn't take much to destroy it now and she was exactly the type of woman who could rip it to shreds.

"The point is..." He trailed off. How could he articulate his tumultuous emotions without revealing just how deeply entangled he was in this game of duplicitous love? "I need to be careful."

She frowned slightly. "Careful? Why? Of what? Me?" Her voice held genuine surprise, making him wonder if she could know why he took such a deep interest in her at all. She was a smart woman. Smarter than she let on. It wouldn't be too hard for her to see right through him.

However, his attraction for her made lying easy because he wasn't acting. He liked her in ways he hadn't enjoyed a woman in a long while. It bothered him that he wanted her on the most primal level. He tried telling himself that he needed to keep her close. But did he? Really? No. He wanted her. Pure and simple.

"Because...." He searched for words that wouldn't betray too much but also wouldn't sound too hollow. "Because I don't want to hurt you. Perhaps I've gone too far. I like you. I'm attracted to you. But I'm a hot mess and can't jump into a relationship. I'm afraid if we continue, all I'll do is hurt your feelings and that's the last thing I want to do."

A soft laugh escaped her lips, like wind chimes tinkering in a gentle breeze. "Hurt me? Relationship?"

Stormi stepped closer, wrapping an arm around his neck. The proximity set his senses on fire, hydrochloric acid to his paper heart. "I invited you in for a drink. Maybe that leads to something in the bedroom. But that doesn't equate to me getting hurt or us having emotional ties. I don't get attached that easily, and I'm not looking. One bad marriage was enough, thank you very much."

She was a hell of a lot more than he bargained for. He should say good night and walk out that door. Only his lips were too close to hers and the scent of her mingling with the cool night air until it was an intoxicating blend sent him over the edge. He inhaled greedily. He looked down into her eyes, vibrant depths of hazel green and gold that had a hint of mischief. She was waiting for him to make the leap.

"I wouldn't want to presume anything," he began, his voice barely above a whisper. "We've both suffered through bad relationships and equally bad breakups."

Her grip around his neck tightened slightly and she moved in fractionally closer, her lips parting in a small smile. "Then don't presume."

He felt her warm breath against his cheek, sending shivers down his spine, and then she pressed her mouth gently against his ear.

"Just enjoy tonight," she whispered. "That's all you need to care about right now. We'll figure out tomorrow when the sun comes up."

Her words were dangerously seductive yet held an

inevitable truth that felt almost comforting to his troubled thoughts. For once, he could switch off his cautious mind and surrender to the moment. He shouldn't. But the temptation was too great. Too powerful to ignore.

"As long as it doesn't hurt you," he found himself saying and there was a hint of desperation in his voice that he didn't try to conceal. "And you won't regret it in the morning."

She pulled back slightly, looking deep into his eyes. "I won't," she replied simply. "Nor should you."

And with that final assurance, he allowed her to coax him farther into the house, shutting the door behind them with a muted thud, leaving the dark night behind.

They stood in the dim light of the hallway, a brief moment of awkward stillness punctuated by the rhythmic *tick-tock* of a grandfather clock somewhere deeper in the house. A war raged inside Lincoln's mind and soul. This was a woman, if he dared strip away the pretense of demanded lies, whom he could honestly care about.

But that was the rub. There was nothing honest in this dance. Except maybe the emotion that drew them together.

When he thought about it, that was the deadliest part of it all—not the lies, nor the danger that might lay ahead, but the emotion. The raw, unfiltered passion that threatened to consume him whole every time her gaze met his. The kind of tenderness that made a man reckless... vulnerable.

In a desperate attempt to control his racing heart, Lincoln focused on the sound of the ticking clock. *Thump-thump. Thump-thump.*

"Would you like that drink?" She broke the silence, her eyes never leaving his. Her question was simple, yet held a complexity that mirrored their current situation.

"No," he replied, his voice soft yet sharp, a contradiction that spoke volumes, hopefully only to him.

She nodded, rewarding him with an innocent and inviting smile. Moving away from him, she headed toward the living room, leaving him to follow her like a moth drawn to a flame. The house was as deceptive as its owner—on the surface, it was rustic, charming even—but underneath, there was an undercurrent of mystery and allure that reflected clearly in its mistress.

He watched as she moved gracefully across the room, every step building up the anticipation within him. His heart pounded against his chest as she turned to face him again, that same mysterious smile playing on her lips. "Shall we?"

Unable to resist any longer, Lincoln closed the distance between them in three strides. He wrapped his arms around her waist and pulled her flush against him. "We shall," he whispered into her ear before capturing her lips with his own. He told himself that he could separate the woman from the job. That the sex was something they both wanted. The attraction was mutual; therefore, he wasn't doing anything wrong.

His body believed the lie.

His mind did not.

The kiss was explosive—a fusion of pent-up longing and raw emotion that set his world ablaze. Her fingers threaded through his hair as their bodies moved in perfect harmony to an unheard rhythm. The air grew thick with desire as they lost themselves in each other, the outside world of death and betrayal forgotten.

Her touch ignited a wildfire within him that he hadn't felt in years—a feeling he never thought he could experience again after six months of refuge in solitude. All caution was thrown away as Lincoln succumbed to the spell she had cast over him and the promise of a night filled with passion and desire—overriding his internal alarms warning him of the possible consequences.

And there would be a price to pay.

They moved deeper into the house and away from the world's prying eyes, completely surrendering to the intoxicating pull between them. Tonight, there were no masks, no lies—only two souls lost in a dance of seduction and undeniable lust.

"This house seems to go on forever," he murmured as he pulled her shirt over her head. He stared at her alluring body, glistening in the moonlight seeping in through the windowpane.

"Bedroom's right here." Stormi pushed open the door. Inside was nothing more than a bed and a chest of drawers. There were no pictures on the walls or even on the dresser. There was nothing to say a full-blooded woman lived in this house. Just furniture and clothing.

Nothing more, nothing less.

Lincoln knew this life all too well. He understood it because he lived it. She was a shell of a woman she once knew. All that existed now were binary digits. The energy flowed from her fingertips to a keyboard and through the digital walls that she desired to puncture in her quest for answers. Now all he wanted to do was fill Stormi's world with something more. Something magical.

Only, all he had to offer her was more lies. More deception. At the end of his tunnel was a truth that she might never forgive him for, if he ever got the chance to even come clean.

He laid her down on the bed and shed the rest of their clothing, ignoring the faint whisper of a conscience.

If he hadn't still been working for Samantha, Stormi would have been just another woman that his good buddy's wife introduced him to. It would have been that simple. The outcome might have been the same. They still might have gone their separate ways, but it wouldn't have left such a bitter taste.

He kissed her neck and whispered how beautiful

she was in her ear. He desperately wanted things to be different because the reality was—he cared. In the span of a few short days, he'd developed feelings.

That was always the way with him. Hard and fast. He couldn't help his DNA if he tried.

Stormi gasped softly under his touch, her eyes shining with unbridled passion and unwavering trust.

Trust that he didn't deserve.

Trust that shouldn't be given and deep down, he suspected, she knew she shouldn't be handing it over to him on a silver platter. Her offer to help wasn't pure, and he knew that. Something he also had to grapple with.

Her gaze held not an iota of judgment—only a deep understanding that seemed to say she knew him far beyond his facade. It was a mirror to his soul, a beacon in the stormy sea of his life. This blend of vulnerability and strength was intoxicating, pulling him deeper into her and further away from his guilt.

The room filled with the mixed scent of rain and passion, a heady concoction that heightened their senses even more. The flickering candlelight cast shadows on their entwined bodies, enhancing the lull in the storm outside.

Lincoln traced his fingers over the curve of her body, memorizing each line and crease as if it were a sacred scripture. He kissed her deeply, his tongue seeking hers in a slow, sensual dance. Their bodies moved in rhythm to a music only they could hear, each touch setting them on fire.

Threading his fingers through her hair, he looked deep into her eyes. "Stormi," he breathed out her name like a prayer. And for once, Lincoln wished he felt at peace amid all the chaos of his life.

He held her closer as they descended deeper into their blissful oblivion. His heart pounded against his chest like a drum echoing throughout the silent room. He was doomed. Destined to go to hell. When she learned who he was and what he knew, she'd hate him.

Hell, he already hated himself.

"What are you thinking?" Stormi asked suddenly, her voice a soft whisper against his ear.

Lincoln paused momentarily, feeling the weight of all his secrets bearing down on him. But looking at Stormi's face glowing softly in the dim light—trusting, open, loving—he found he couldn't bring himself to break her heart. Not just yet.

Besides, she had her own secrets to bear.

"Nothing," he murmured back with feigned nonchalance, hoping his voice didn't betray the storm of emotions raging within him. "Nothing at all."

As they lay in her bed, Lincoln had only one thought. A fucked-up thought, but it was one he couldn't shake and that was—this was right; this was where he was meant to be. Despite the lies, despite the secrets, in her arms, he found a home, a sanctuary. And tonight, he had no intention of leaving that behind.

CHAPTER SEVEN

Stormi watched as Lincoln eased from her bed, hiking up his jeans, and tiptoeing out of her bedroom. The sun had barely begun to cast its morning glow through the window, but early morning regrets had already filled her aching heart.

Lincoln was like no other man she'd ever met. Ignore his sexy swagger and rich accent that would make any woman with a pulse drool. His boyish good looks and charming personality were only minute aspects of the man. While they obviously served him well, it was his unmatched intelligence that would have her swooning until the cows came home.

Of all the insane things Stormi's ever done over the years, letting Lincoln spend the night had to be one of the dumbest. It was a mistake that kept on giving.

Besides, having to sneak out of her bedroom to lock her office, praying that Lincoln hadn't already seen the five screens and three computers, there was the fact that she lived like a freak.

Her family room consisted of a sofa, a chair, and a television. Her kitchen had a table, two chairs, and well, that was about it. The living room had a piano. Nothing else. And she didn't even know how to play the stupid thing. Her bedroom, how fucking pathetic.

She was worse than a twenty-year-old college male living in his first apartment, minus the dogs playing poker wall hanging. Either she looked like a terrorist or a cliché for a sad, spinster, hacker chick with no life.

Both equally piteous in their own ways.

All she wanted to do was get a second date, gain his trust, get close, and hopefully, he'd start talking more about his job. She needed answers. To understand what was happening inside Zero Gravity. And how best to find the data she knew without a doubt would exonerate her father.

She flung her arm over her eyes and groaned as she listened to the sound of footsteps approaching.

And that brought her to the biggest mistake of all. One that she wasn't sure she could even muster up the courage to admit to herself, much less Lincoln. Living a life of celibacy hadn't been difficult. While she found a few men nice to stare at, none had made her want to rip their clothes off and literally play a game of chance with her life.

And theirs.

"Good morning, beautiful," Lincoln said. "I managed to find coffee in your kitchen."

"I usually stop at that little place in town on my way to work."

He tugged at her arm. "I rustled you up some eggs and toast." He chuckled. "You don't eat at home much, do you?"

"I loathe cooking, so it's a lot of takeout." She fluffed the pillow and sat up a little taller, sniffing. "That actually smells kind of good."

"I can do breakfast foods relatively well." He leaned back, crossing his ankles. "I mean, how hard is it to scramble a few eggs and stick bread in a machine? I would have added meat, but you didn't have any." He waved a piece of buttered toast around before shoving half of it in his mouth.

"Yeah, I polished off the microwavable bacon the other day."

"Microwave bacon? Now that's just wrong." He laughed, digging into his eggs. "I don't mean to go all judgmental on you, but why haven't you decorated this place? It's got great potential."

She shrugged, lifting her coffee from the nightstand. "I wasn't sure I was going to stay. My lease is only for four months, which means it's up in two. But my funds are limited and if I don't need it, I don't spend money on it. Honestly, this place is too big for me. I keep looking for a smaller rental. A two-bedroom would be perfect. This place has four."

"I noticed that one of them doesn't even have any furniture and the other one is locked."

She laughed. "Yeah, that's where I have some boxes, other furniture, and shit. Just haven't gotten around to it. Out of sight, out of mind."

"I know how that is. If you want a hand, I'm happy to help out."

"You're a regular Boy Scout." That was the last thing she needed. She shoveled in the last of her eggs and set the plate aside. Lifting her cell, she checked the time. She didn't want to be rude, but she did have some work she wanted to do before heading in for the paying job.

"What are your plans for the day?" he asked.

"Just work. You?" A sense of dread filled her belly. Now that she'd had sex with him, she had no idea how to behave and she really needed to figure that out. She also needed to deal with a heavy dose of honesty. The man did have a right to know she wasn't taking birth control.

And that they hadn't used any.

Or maybe that conversation could wait a few days.

"I've got a meeting this morning, and then I was going to head to the library to do some research." He lifted her chin. "Do you still want to help me?"

"I thought you said you couldn't discuss your work." She swallowed. Hard. She had never been good at reading people. Kara had been quick to point out that had been her downfall when it came to her husband, Kurt. He'd been a master manipulator. He was good at pulling the wool over most people's eyes. He was also a million-dollar salesman. The worst part had been that Stormi had fallen for his lies.

Every single one of them.

With Lincoln, she didn't know what his agenda was, except he was dangerous because of the skills he possessed. But she'd covered her tracks. The worst thing that could happen at this point was he knew she'd spied on him. She'd have to come up with a reason why and another for why she possessed those skills.

"I can't. So, as long as you're willing to do some grunt work without being able to ask any questions, I'll gladly take your help. That way I can focus my efforts on some other things."

"Oh, sounds very spy-ish." She rubbed her hands together. "Research is my all-time favorite thing to do."

"Now, that sounds like someone who reads too much." He batted her nose. "I wish I could tell you what I was doing. It would certainly make my life easier, especially if I'm going to have you help me. But my boss—"

"You mean your ex-girlfriend."

"Please don't remind me of that technicality." He let out a long breath. "Samantha gets very weird about jobs and security, so if she knew, she'd probably fire me, which wouldn't be the end of the world." He winked. "But the bigger picture is my client. I'm dealing with proprietary information. I can't let outside—"

"Now that I actually understand and you don't have to say another word. Just let me know how I can help. Honestly, sometimes I get bored at my job. If I can do anything outside of stacking books and keeping teenagers from having sex in the private rooms, it would make my day."

He jerked his head back. "You've caught people doing the nasty in those rooms?"

"Oh, I have." She waggled her finger. "And no. It's never been Tal and Heather's kids."

"I know what I want to do on your lunch break." He cupped her breast, fanning his thumb over her nipple.

"Not going to happen, big fella." She patted his chest. "I caught them before the act because we have cameras."

He chuckled. "And I know how to disable them."

She blinked. So did she, but she wasn't going to let him know that. "Um, still not happening."

"Can't blame a guy for trying," he said. "What time do you get off work tonight?"

"Six. Why?"

"I just thought I'd cook you dinner at my place."

She palmed her coffee, staring at the dark liquid. She'd made a big deal last night about no relationships. That this was sex. Nothing more. She didn't want to come off as needy, but she didn't want to insult or blow him off either. "I want you to know that I had a really great time last night and I certainly wouldn't mind it happening again. But—"

He pressed his finger over her lips. "It's dinner. To talk about work. Or anything you might have found. And I'm glad you had fun. I did too and it will happen again. However, there are no strings. But I'll either be buried in my own research or back at my home office writing lines and lines of code, while I leave you to do crappy work for me. Which I intend to pay you for. So, dinner would be more work-related than pleasure. It's just that I can't afford to discuss work in public and I don't want anyone to know I've asked you to help me. Are you okay with that?"

She nodded.

"Okay. So, your assignment for the day is to go through the science and engineering periodicals and dig up articles about Zero Gravity and other space-flight companies regarding their technology on their rocket boosters."

Her eyes burned. "Are you looking for anything specific?"

"That's the thing about research. I don't know exactly what I'm searching for. So, keep it broad."

"That's not going to make my part in this easy." She adjusted the comforter. "You've got to have some sort of parameter. I've helped a lot of students over the years with research papers and without a theme, mission statement, or even a question that needs answering, it's nearly impossible for me to set them up with the right books on the right topic."

"All right. Why don't you search for all spaceflights that have failed. Find the reasons for those failures and then look at how those tasked with private spaceflight are going to ensure they don't. Try not to get specific with which engineer said what. Or who has what patent. Or even who works for what company. I just want the specifics on how the boosters work. What tests they go through to ensure they won't fail."

"Do you want me to compare and contrast in a blind study?"

"You keep talking sexy like that and I'm going to ravish you and miss my meeting." He nestled himself between her legs, kissing her lips, hard. His tongue twirled around in her mouth as if she were his last meal.

She clasped her ankles around his waist.

He groaned. "I shouldn't start what I can't finish."

"You Brits are such teases." She released him. "I'm sure I can manage your task for the day. Anything else in case I finish?"

"If you do, text me. I have an entire list of shit that I need to look into, but what you find might change my next course of action." He eased off the bed and palmed her cheek. "You're a special woman, Stormi."

"You're sweet to say that."

"It's the truth." He kissed her forehead. "I'll see you

later." He snagged his shirt and strolled out of the bedroom like he didn't have a care in the world.

She leaped from the mattress, wrapped her robe around her half-naked body, and raced to the front window. It seemed like it took forever for him to round the corner toward Zeke's bar.

Quickly, she locked the front door, grabbed a second cup of coffee, and made a beeline for her office. She fired up her main computer, running her safety protocols, making sure no one had tried to hack into her system. Satisfied she was alone in her world, she set out to find all she could on one Pamela Stokes, waitress extraordinaire.

Stormi started with a basic Google search—something simple and easy that anyone and their toddler could do. It always amazed her how much she could find out about a person simply by typing their name in a search bar.

Pam had followed her boyfriend, who, unfortunately, had landed a job at Zero Gravity.

Just Stormi's fucking luck.

Ross Grayson worked in the public relations department.

According to Pam's social media, the breakup had been a shock. She'd posted images of herself moving, but Ross wasn't in many of those pictures. As Stormi did a deeper dive—or, in reality, hacked Pam's email—she learned that Ross had told Pam not to come. That he wanted some time and space.

A break from the relationship. He called her needy. Possessive. And that if they were going to even have half a chance, she needed to back off.

She didn't listen and less than a month after being here, Ross not only sent her a scathing email, but he told her he was dating someone else.

Ouch.

Stormi actually felt a little sorry for Pam.

She worked her way backward through Pam's life until she landed in her hometown of Lake George, New York.

Fuck.

Pam had attended prep school down in Albany, so they never went to the same high school, but they were only two years apart. Their paths were sure to have crossed at some point before Stormi's father had moved her away. Not to mention the scandal that had rocked Saratoga when she'd been arrested.

Didn't matter it was under a different name. Stormi could cut her hair and change the color, but if anyone cared to look close enough, they'd see her for who she really was and that's Amanda Norris.

Stormi leaned back and let out a long breath. Under normal circumstances, this warranted a call to Kara, her handler. But Kara hadn't wanted her to move to Fallport to begin with. Kara had warned her it was a mistake. Too many people connected to her father. It only took one person to make the connection and her cover would be blown.

Kurt wanted revenge.

But Stormi wasn't afraid of her husband. She should be terrified of the people he did business with, but for three years, there wasn't a single ounce of chatter.

No. She wasn't going to call Kara. Not about this. Not yet. Besides, Pam followed her boyfriend. She came long before Stormi did. Stormi didn't need to worry about Pam. But she would keep an eye on what the woman was doing. Just to be safe.

However, today, she would indulge in research and then tonight, she'd escape in Lincoln's arms while forging a new plan.

One that included telling Lincoln the truth.

Or some version of it that wouldn't have him hating her in the end.

CHAPTER EIGHT

Lincoln leaned against the hood of Tal's old Jeep and stared at Stormi's house. He couldn't help but wonder what her life might be like if her father hadn't died. Would she have stayed in South Florida working in a bookstore?

He chuckled. At least her love of books was real.

But he wanted to know more about what she'd been like before she'd made the decision to turn her life into an obsession. To have a singular goal and nothing else.

His cell buzzed. He snagged it from his back pocket. "Hey, Tal."

"She's neatly tucked in the library," Tal said. "Are you sure you want to do this?"

"Yup."

"Not a good way to start a relationship," Tal said.

Lincoln scoffed. "We had sex. And for the record, I'm not the only one telling lies here. So is she."

"For good reason."

"I have valid ones too and let's remember, I can't come out and tell her I know her true identity. Not unless her life is in danger, and even then, I'll work to keep that juicy nugget a secret."

"Suit yourself, but don't say I didn't warn you." The line went dead.

Which was fine with Lincoln. Right now, he wished he hadn't confided in Tal to begin with. He waited ten minutes before hacking into her system, ensuring any security she had in place was turned off. He loathed himself as he shimmied open the back door.

Her house couldn't be called a home. It was merely four walls in which she came in from the storm that was her life. As he made his way through the kitchen and family room, he searched for something—anything—that hinted at a soul, but he found nothing.

Stormi was lost to the shadows of her past. The person she pretended to be was a cardboard cutout, a doll she dressed up and played with when she was forced to be present in the life someone else, namely the government, had chosen for her. But the other person lurking in her mind's dark recesses no longer existed.

She couldn't. And not just because she'd unwillingly helped her husband commit a crime and then turned on him, but because that woman had lost everything she thought she held dear. The only thing left was the memory of who she believed her father to be and the drive to ensure his legacy wouldn't be ruined for eternity.

Lincoln suspected her motivation stemmed from guilt and was fueled by a desire to right all the wrongs she'd done in her old life regarding the one person she loved but, for whatever reason, had stopped communicating with.

He understood regrets. He had a few. But none of them were worth dwelling on. Change one event, and his entire life might be different, and if he were being honest with himself, his life didn't suck. He sighed. He wasn't so sure what Stormi thought of hers, though. She had a decent sense of humor and she appeared to be grounded. But her house was depressingly empty, and here he thought he was a minimalist.

But at least he had pictures. People. Things he cared about.

He lived his life outside of the inner workings of technology. Hell, he thrived in a world that didn't necessarily rely on all things techie. He had a healthy passion for the outside world. He knew how to shut down and get one with nature. The Royal Navy had taught him the balance between the two worlds. They demanded both his brains and his brawn. He had to be mentally sharp as well as a trained killer.

He was a walking oxymoron.

It was something that Samantha never quite understood. If she wasn't in front of her computers, she wasn't living. The idea of going for a leisurely walk made the woman break out in hives. Relaxing to her was hacking into the neighbor's computer to see what kind of porn they watched.

Picking the lock of what he believed was Stormi's home office, he pushed all those thoughts out of his head and focused on his morning agenda. It would be easier to upload his spyware at the source so he could see inside her system and keep tabs on what she was doing, instead of doing it the hard way, like he had to this morning. That meant he might only get bits and pieces.

He might have missed that Pam was from her hometown or how Stormi had dug a little deeper than she should have into how connected Pam might be to her past and present. That pricked his skin for a variety of reasons. He didn't believe in coincidences, but Pam had been living in this town for a year.

Stormi two months.

No one could have predicted Stormi would move to Fallport. She could have chosen any number of locations close by. But it didn't take a genius to consider the possibility that she'd look into her father's death.

However, that meant someone had to believe she was alive.

Lincoln also had to consider that Stormi and Pam had not crossed paths, which was also odd, but not really. According to Tal, Stormi really didn't get out much—actually, not at all.

He pushed open the door and a smile tugged at his

lips as a sense of pride filled his chest. He ran his fingers across her desk before pulling out her chair. He tapped the keyboard, and two of the screens crackled to life.

This was the ultimate betrayal and she'd never forgive him for it, if she found out.

He inserted the drive and hit the necessary keystrokes to start his program. Glancing at his watch, he noted the time. He needed fifteen minutes. Tal would alert him if there was any sign of her coming home. However, the library was set to open in two minutes.

Lincoln was safe.

That was until the screen froze and his code got hung up.

"Shit," he mumbled. Probably some extra special firewall that she'd written herself. He should have been prepared for that. He scanned the last line of code, working backward until he found the stop line.

Holy shit. Leaning forward, he studied the coding. No way. It couldn't be. He hadn't seen this work in years. Four, to be exact. And he'd only come across it twice. The first time had been when the British government had butted heads with an American security company. The only reason he'd even been remotely familiar with this particular code had been because someone had created a back door.

But it hadn't been the creator who had done that.

He knew this because the coding had been vastly different.

The second time he'd seen it was when Samantha had asked him to look at something similar three years ago. Again, a back door was written vastly different from the original coder. That was never good.

He pushed those thoughts out of his head for the time being as he wormed his way into her system and rewrote her code so his program could continue to run. But he also added two lines, ensuring that his software wouldn't halt again.

Only, three minutes later, a popup appeared on the screen with a dialogue box.

I know who you are and what you did last summer.

Lincoln chuckled. He folded his arms across his chest and watched while she tried to stop his hack. She was good, but unfortunately, her keystrokes were not fast enough and the Wi-Fi at the library not strong enough. Even if she was on a hardwired computer, she wouldn't be able to catch up.

"Well, fuck." He leaned forward as he caught the one line she managed to insert.

A kill code.

"Not going to happen, sweetheart." He cracked his knuckles and removed the line, but noticed the code was broken. "Oh, you're a sneaky little devil." Had he not done something similar on a previous job for the Special Boat Service, he might have missed the attempt to distract him while she worked on shutting her system down. "Sorry, babe. Time to give you the boot." He managed to cut her off at the pass. Before he shoved her all the way off, he decided to leave her with a parting message. It was a calculated risk and it could totally backfire on him, but it would be interesting to see what she did.

In fifteen minutes, you'll be able to access your system. I'm of no threat to you. But what you are doing is dangerous. I can't do my job and protect you if you get in my way.

He logged her off and locked her out while he finished loading the software. Not only would this give him the ability to watch everything she did, but now he'd have full access to her files. He'd be able to see what she had on Zero Gravity, and her father.

He was going to hell, that was for damn sure.

It didn't matter that he told himself he was doing this for her own protection, because that was utter bullshit. Sure, he did want to keep her safe, and this was one way to go about it. However, the reality was he needed information, and this was just one more way to get it.

After shutting everything down, he locked the door and exited out the back. No sooner was he climbing behind the wheel of his Jeep than his cell buzzed.

Unknown Caller

Well, shit.

"This is Lincoln Walsh. Who do I have the pleasure of speaking with?"

"This is Special Agent Kara Martin with the FBI."

Interesting. "And what does the FBI want with a retired Royal Navy guy from the UK?"

"That's funny, because you came looking for me through an old colleague of mine. A woman by the name of Fenmore Ford."

"That's right. I did." He turned the key over and punched the gas. He had twenty-two minutes to make it to his meeting with a different agent. "My line is secure, is yours?"

"It is," she said. "But I'm not comfortable mentioning certain names."

"I don't believe we need to." He glanced in his rearview mirror. While he had no reason to believe he would be followed, his paranoia was at an all-time high. Besides, Jimmy asked him to take an odd route out of town, and to double-check, just in case. Lincoln respected the badge. And he didn't want to do anything that would jeopardize Stormi or her father. "Do you have any idea what she's up to?"

"Why am I speaking to you?"

"Because I was hired to fix Zero Gravity's security problem," Lincoln said. "And I found her in their digital hallway."

"Does she know this?"

"She knows someone saw her and my guess is she's trying to figure out if that someone is me." Lincoln didn't trust many people, but Darius told him that if push came to shove, Kara would be on the right side, which didn't always mean she'd follow the rules.

That was a good thing.

"Only, I don't want her to know for sure it's me, and I want her to stop poking around Zero Gravity. I need you to make that happen."

Kara laughed, but it wasn't a funny ha-ha kind of laugh. "Look. She's well within the program to be living and doing what she wants."

"Um, I believe this constitutes illegal actively. She changed some of her history and—"

"Don't tell me this shit. I don't want to know. If she's living her life as a bookworm with the identity that was created for her, I don't care. As far as what she might be doing that could be affecting what you've been hired to do, well, I have one question for you."

"And what's that?"

"Is it possible that Dante Norris was set up to take the fall?"

"Can I get back to you on that?" Lincoln pulled into the old motel on the outskirts of town, put the car into park, and pinched the bridge of his nose.

"I'm asking because when Fenmore reached out, it got me thinking. Got my husband's mind spinning too," Kara said. "It seems like you're taking your sweet time with their new security cyber system and that makes me wonder if maybe my girl wasn't onto something. But what really got my panties in a twist was learning there was a connection to Fallport and a one Agent James Hallenbeck. After doing a tiny bit of digging, I found out he's been researching Zero Gravity. Any idea why that might be?"

"I haven't the foggiest," Lincoln said with a slight hint of humor to his voice. "But perhaps we can work on our communication skills."

"That might be a moral imperative."

"I'll be in touch about that because I also need a little more information regarding why our friend is in the predicament she's in and it might be related to my current employment," Lincoln said.

"That's cryptic. Care to elaborate?"

"Let's just say my employer once had me look at coding that matched her underground name a few years ago, but it had been fucked with by a different coder."

"That makes me wonder what your employer knows and that's fucked up for a whole different set of reasons," Kara said. "Would Darius and Fenmore be able to get us both what we need?"

"I'm sure they would," Lincoln said. "Do you think you can get our mutual friend to stand down and stay out of my way for the time being?"

"She has never once listened to me except for one thing and that was to sever all ties to her past. She's done that."

"Not really. She's still hacking and you use her for that," he said. "Every hacker, even an ethical one, has a language. You can see it in their coding. I saw her system today and while I might be considered a genius, anyone with half a brain would have known that the woman behind those computer screens was known as Twister in the hacker world. If I can pick up on that in fifteen minutes, my boss could have picked up on that in half that time."

"Maybe it's time I pluck her right the fuck out of Virginia."

"Nope. I can protect her and she can help me. If we can get her to stay out of Zero Gravity until I'm ready for her to go in."

"You want to use her?"

Lincoln checked his watch. "I've got a meeting in three minutes. Trust me. She'll want to be part of this. And so will you. But right now, there are a few different parts that aren't moving in the same direction. I need to pull them all together. Will you help me?"

"Fuck me," Kara muttered. "If Darius didn't work with a few people I know who are the best in the world, I'd tell you to go screw yourself. That and our friend is the kind of person who will go it alone because she doesn't feel like she has anyone in her corner."

"She's got me," Lincoln said. "I'll be in touch." Now all he had to do was convince Jimmy that working with him and Kara was a good idea.

CHAPTER NINE

If Stormi wasn't so damn interested in why Lincoln wanted the information on failed rocket boosters and all the rigorous testing these companies went through, she wouldn't bother. Not after catching the asshole red-handed in her computer system.

After they'd slept together.

What a fucking jerk.

Of course, she couldn't say anything. If she did, she'd have a lot of explaining to do.

What made it all worse was Kara's text message asking her—no, telling her—to stay away from Zero Gravity. All that did was make Stormi wonder what Lincoln was really up to and if she should confide in him, but when she pushed Kara into asking why, all Kara had to say was that she'd heard through her internal sources that things were happening.

Stormi didn't have anyone in her life whom she

trusted, except Kara, though trust was a strong word when it came to Kara and the FBI. Sure, Kara had made it possible for Stormi to stay out of prison. She'd also helped her start a new life. She even gave her enough rope to hang herself. But now she was begging her to take a major step back instead of turning a blind eye.

Well, Stormi wasn't sure she could do that. For now, she'd leave the computer shit alone. At least until she learned what the hell Lincoln had installed in her system. And she'd find out soon enough.

She flipped through the pages of one of the books she'd pulled from the shelves. So far, she hadn't learned anything new in her research. It was difficult not to focus on Zero Gravity and her father's work on rocket boosters. But she did her best to look up every article and book on the topic.

And there were plenty.

Thankfully, the library had been quiet most of the day.

She glanced up from her notebook. "Oh, hello, Marisa. Brad. How are you two doing today?"

"Better than my little brother," Marisa said. "He's still grounded, which is why we're here. The only way my folks would let him come was if we acted as chaperones."

"That's awfully nice of the two of you," Stormi said, glancing around. She smiled. "I see he found Suzie already. Should I be worried that I'm aiding and abetting?"

"Oh, no." Brad shook his head. "They are allowed to see each other. Suzie's mom knows Chad is here."

"We're under strict orders to make sure they don't sneak out." Marisa laughed. "Because we've never done anything like that before."

Stormi leaned forward and rested her arms on the counter. "Do not put me in a position where I have to be a nasty adult."

"We wouldn't dream of it," Brad said. "But we were hoping we could use one of the rooms with a television to watch a movie?"

Stormi cocked her head. "Just so the two of you know, there are security cameras in those rooms and I'm going to have to ask you to leave the door open." She waggled her finger.

"Seriously, Stormi." Marisa shook her head. "Do all adults over twenty think teenagers are sex-starved crazy people? We just want to watch *Aquaman* while those two lovebirds over there try to find a corner to steal a kiss or two."

"For the record, yes. That's not what we think. That's what we know." Stormi snagged the keys to the room closest to the front desk. "I know five girls from my high school who were pregnant before graduation."

"Ew, gross. I don't need this lecture from you," Marisa said. "It's bad enough my father leaves pamphlets around and tries to have the sex talk with me all the time."

"At least your dad cares enough to try." Stormi unlocked the door.

"She's right. I mean, my dad and I talk about stuff like that, but my mom?" Brad let out a long breath. "Her idea of the big talk was to tell me that if I dared knock a girl up, I could kiss the family fortune goodbye. Then she tossed a box of condoms at me and told me to check the expiration date."

"I hope the two of you—"

"We're not having sex," Marisa said with red cheeks. "Not that it's any of your business."

"Perhaps it's not. But if you ever want a grown-up to talk to who's not your mother, though moms know best, I'm here." Stormi smiled. "Enjoy the movie."

"Thanks, Stormi." Marisa nodded.

Stormi totally overstepped a dozen lines. But she didn't regret doing it. Marisa and Brad were good kids. And they were lucky to have parents who had open discussions about adult topics that would inevitably affect them sooner rather than later. But that didn't mean other people in their lives couldn't interject some wisdom.

She made her way back behind the counter and eyed Chad and Suzie, who were currently preparing for story time which would begin in twenty minutes. Suzie was gifted when it came to reading to small children. She was animated and had a way with voice inflection. Stormi had learned that one day she wanted to be a teacher. She'd make for a good one.

Chad, on the other hand, was not as good, but he was working on it, and Stormi enjoyed watching him try.

Ah, young love.

The thought immediately soured her mood. Her emotions had gotten the better of her when it came to Lincoln. His company had been hired to implement a new cybersecurity system. She'd learned that the man could write that code in his sleep.

So what the hell was he dicking around for?

Oh yeah. He was trying to find her and now that he had, what was he going to do? He had to know she'd been the one; otherwise, why go to her house and hack her system? What was his end game? Have her arrested? Did he know who she was and had been in contact with Kara?

If that were the case, Kara would have pulled her, or at least that's what Stormi wanted to believe.

She should run.

And fast.

That was still an option.

"Excuse me." A woman who appeared to be in her early forties approached. She wore red capri slacks with a white top. Her long brown hair touched her shoulders. It was thick and straight but had a bit of bounce to it. The woman had piercing blue eyes and flawless skin.

Stormi blinked as a tickle of recognition flowed through her mind. Shit. She was staring at none other than Jeannie Mooney, Norman's soon-to-be ex-wife, better known as David Caulkin's daughter.

"Yes. Can I help you with something?" Stormi had never met Jeannie before, but she had met her father and her husband when she was in high school. The encounters had been brief. A few times at company picnics and Mr. Caulkin had been to her father's home a couple of times.

What she remembered about Norman was he never seemed to fit in with the rest of the people at the company parties and he didn't hang out with her father. According to what she'd learned after meeting Brad, his father worked in the marketing department and had very little to do with engineering or research and development. His role was to make promotional videos and from what she saw on the internet and television, he seemed to do that well.

"I've been on the hunt for a certain book. I've tried finding a used copy of it online and in used bookstores, but I haven't been successful. I was told at a different library that you have a copy of it." The woman dug into her purse. "Do you have it?" Jeannie slid a piece of paper across the counter.

"As a matter of fact, we do." Stormi closed the book and held it up. "Oddly, I was just thumbing through it."

"Really? Now what interest would aerodynamics and spaceflight have on a librarian?"

"Oh, I'm interested in all books." Stormi smiled.

"Are you looking to check this out? If so, I'll just need your library card."

"I don't have one of those. Is it really necessary?"

Stormi nodded. "All I need is a valid driver's license and I can hook you up in no time."

"That would be splendid." With a delicate touch, Jeannie handed over her ID. She tapped her fingernails on the wood surface and waited, impatiently, while Stormi keyed in the information.

In these situations, Stormi would normally take her sweet time, but she didn't want to spend a single second longer with the likes of Jeannie. Besides the stories she'd heard from Heather and Tal about the way she treated Norman and Brad, the woman appeared to be a stuck-up snob. Not to mention, her father and their company killed Stormi's dad.

So there was that.

"Here you go." Stormi stuck the printout inside the book. "The return date is on that paper. There are late fees, so if you want to avoid those, give us a call if you need to keep it longer. Unless someone is on the wait-list for this bad boy, I doubt it will be a problem." Oh, she'd make sure she put someone's name down for the book, but only because she wanted it back.

For Lincoln's sake.

Right.

"Thank you." Jeannie turned and gasped.

"Mom. What are you doing here?" Brad stood five feet away with his mouth gaping open.

“I should be asking you that,” Jeannie said. “You’re supposed to be at your father’s this week.”

“I am.” Brad folded his arms. “He’s at work, like he does every day, and you’re supposed to be out of town. Or at least that’s what you told us.”

“I was, but I came back a few days early.” She inched closer, reaching out, resting her hand on Brad’s shoulder.

He shrugged it away.

“I had some things I needed to do for your grandfather.” She tapped the book. “Finding this was one of them. Would you like to go grab some lunch?”

Brad shook his head. “I’m here with friends, and then Dad and I have plans.”

“All right and perhaps it’s best if you didn’t tell your father you saw me here today. You know how he gets.”

“Yeah. Sure. No problem.”

“Love you, honey.” She kissed his cheek.

Brad let out a long breath. “So, you got to meet my mother. She’s a real gem, isn’t she.” He rolled his eyes.

“I’m going to stick my nose where it doesn’t belong for the second time today, but she’s the only mother you’ll ever have. Whatever problems you’re having now, I know they seem massive, but take it from someone who lost her parents young, cut her a little slack.”

“Trust me, I’ve given her many chances. Forgiven a ton of stuff. I don’t even care that she cheated on my dad. That’s between them. My problem is she doesn’t care about me. All she cares about is what my grandfather thinks and whether or not he's going to leave her any money." Brad leaned against the counter. "When she found out I wanted to go to the Air Force Academy, she laughed. She told me that we could afford for me to go to any college I wanted and to forget about the military. I was too good for that."

Oh boy. Stormi should really bite her fucking tongue. But she couldn't. "You know, my dad and I fought like there was no tomorrow. The two things we fought about most was my boyfriend, whom I married to spite him, and my choice in careers."

"He didn't like you being a librarian?"

"Nope." God, she was getting too good at lying. And to a kid no less. "He wanted me to do something big with my life. He thought maybe I should be a doctor. Or a lawyer. Or work with computers. Anything but something so traditional as what I do. He also hated my husband, although he turned out to be right about that one."

"I didn't know you had ever been married."

"It's not something I talk about," she said. "But my point is, all my dad wanted was the best for me, but he often went about it in such a way that it made me rebel. It got so bad that when he died, we were barely speaking to each other and that's something that I will always regret."

"It's hard to have a conversation with someone who is never around or constantly pawns me off on someone else." Brad raised his hand. "Not that mind. I love living with my dad. Don't get me wrong, he can be a pain in my ass, especially when it comes to me and Marisa. He thinks we're too young to be this serious, but at least he's willing to get to know her and be present in my life. My mom, on the other hand, won't listen to anything. She's going to be in for a rude awakening when I actually leave for the academy this summer."

"What does your dad think about all that?"

"It's not his first choice for me, but he supports it." Brad squared his shoulders and smiled. "He believes it's honorable and I'll get a good education. He tells me what I do with it after that is up to me."

"Well, young man, what do you want to be when you grow up?"

"That, I'm not so sure of yet." Brad laughed. "My grandfather would like me to go work for his company. He thinks my fascination with the Air Force means I want to be a pilot and maybe an astronaut, but I'm leaning more toward a fire protection specialist."

"That's interesting."

"I've always been fascinated by fires and the Air Force would give more than the training necessary to become a firefighter. It's a unique team."

"You sound quite passionate about it," Stormi said.

"Oh my God." Marisa came up behind Brad and rested her head on his shoulder. "You did not get my boyfriend talking about being a fireman, did you? Now he'll never shut up."

Stormi chuckled. "Having something that makes your eyes glow like that isn't a bad thing."

"Maybe not, but he left me alone in that room while he was supposed to be snagging us a couple of waters. For all I knew, he was out here flirting with some other girl."

"That would never happen." Brad kissed her cheek.

"None of that in my library." Stormi waved her hand. "Now get out of my way. I have work to do." She snagged her pencil and jotted down a couple of questions she had about the book she'd given to Jeannie. She had no idea how she was going to inform Lincoln of this tiny little detail, but he had the right to know.

Didn't he?

LINCOLN TAPPED his knuckles against the old wood door. It took thirty seconds before it rattled and opened.

A tall, thin man wearing a badge and a gun peeked his head outside. "I hope you weren't followed."

"I was not," Lincoln said. "I sat in my Jeep across the street for five minutes and then drove around the block to make sure. I checked my vehicle for tracking devices. I'm also a computer genius, so I know there's nothing on my phone or anywhere else on my person."

"I've heard all about you from Fenmore and her husband. My wife's sister also happens to be married to Brayden Gibson."

"He's a good man and I've met Madison. She's sweet."

"That she is and her husband saved mine and my wife's lives. I spoke to him before agreeing to meet with you. He said I could trust you."

"So, then are you going to let me in?"

"We have to agree that what is seen and said here, stays here." Jimmy arched a brow.

"I can live with that."

Jimmy pulled open the door.

Lincoln crossed the threshold and his heart stopped as the door slammed shut. "Of all the things I expected, seeing Dante Norris alive with my own two eyes was not one of them."

"My daughter can't know." Dante stood about six feet tall. He had thin gray hair. Scars and burns lined the side of his face and snaked down the right side of his body. "I'm lucky to have survived that explosion as it is."

"This might be one of the most inappropriate questions I could possibly ask at this time, but when did you learn she was alive?" Lincoln glanced between the two men.

"I've known all along. But he learned about a month ago," Jimmy said.

"But to be fair, I struggled to believe that my child

killed herself. She was a lot of things. Willful. Stubborn. And that child could hold a grudge longer than anyone I know. But suicidal? No. She was too angry for that. And not the kind of angry that led to depression, but the kind that would drive a person to seek answers."

"What her husband did to her was diabolical," Lincoln said. "He ruined her reputation as an ethical hacker. There was no way out for her. I've seen the evidence. Even though she was the one who turned on him, ultimately proving that he also played a part, he managed to put in her coding. It made her look guilty as sin."

"You say that as if you know she didn't do it."

"Because she didn't." Lincoln smiled. "Every coder has a style. Hers is quite unique and he hadn't mastered it."

"Then why did she still go down for the crime even in her death?"

"Because that's what the FBI wanted," Jimmy said. "It was for her protection. Kurt might suspect she's the one who rolled, but if the people he was working for knew, well, they'd be gunning for her too. It was best that they believed the FBI thought she played a role. Not to mention, it helped us force Kurt to take the guilty plea and let us go after his partners, shutting down a ring of crime."

"Not everyone is behind bars." Lincoln cocked his head.

"They will be soon," Jimmy said. "Our field office in Albany is handling them. They've been working on it for three years and they are closing ranks. Trust me, they will be out of the picture in a few weeks. They aren't our problem." Jimmy flipped open his laptop. "Unfortunately, Stormi and you could be."

"I take offense to that statement." Lincoln folded his arms and leaned against the wall.

"You shouldn't. Your computer skills are better than Darius described." Jimmy eased into the chair. "I've been in Zero Gravity's system since Dante over here died."

"Now if I was so good, how the fuck did I miss that?" Lincoln didn't like being made a fool of.

Jimmy pointed to the computer screen.

Lincoln narrowed his stare. "You've got to be fucking kidding me. Does Norman Mooney know you're using his credentials to poke around inside Zero Gravity?"

"He's helping me," Jimmy said.

"Well, fuck me." Lincoln threaded his fingers through his hair. "That adds flavor to this case that puts me between a rock and a hard place. I know that man's kid. He's dating Tal's daughter."

"He's also seen firsthand what his wife and father-in-law are capable of," Dante said. "It's why he left his wife."

"I thought it was because she was cheating on him." Lincoln's brain filled with a million questions. The first one, and most important when it came to his role was, what the hell did his ex-girlfriend know about any of this? Because nothing made sense.

Including her reason for wanting to save face, as she put it.

"That's what he tells people and that's partly true," Jimmy said. "After the explosion, Norman knew something wasn't right. But he doesn't have anything to do with that part of the company."

"Neither does his wife," Lincoln said.

Dante chuckled. "Actually, that's not true. People forget that she has a master's degree in physics. Her father is incredibly old-fashioned and doesn't believe a woman could possibly run his company, much less have the brain power to develop and deploy rocket boosters. He did, however, want her to become entangled with his top scientists or engineers. He was quite disappointed when she married Norman, which I believe she did to piss off the old man and force his hand to let her be the brains when he retired."

"How's that working for her?" Lincoln asked with a heavy dose of sarcasm. God, he hated sexist assholes.

"Jeannie is a smart woman and her talents were underutilized for years," Dante said. "I felt sorry for her and took her under my wing. I often argued with her father about how brilliant her ideas were. It cost me a promotion once, but I kept thinking about how I treated my little girl and I wished I had done things differently."

"What does that mean, exactly?" Lincoln asked.

"I hated her chosen career path," Dante said. "I didn't understand ethical hacking. I thought it was a fancy word for doing something illegal and getting away with it."

"I'm an ethical hacker, for lack of a better word." Lincoln held Dante's unwavering gaze.

"I know better now and I tried making amends with Amanda—I mean Stormi. But her fucking husband is a cockroach." Dante waggled his finger. "Now, that I was right about."

"I won't argue with you on that point." Lincoln nodded. "But I'd like to get back to Jeannie, Norman, and how Stormi and I are a problem for you."

"Your new system will make it impossible for me to poke around as Norman. He won't have the access I need," Jimmy said.

"I can make sure you have whatever you need inside Zero Gravity on a few conditions."

"You're not in a position to negotiate with the FBI." Jimmy leaned back in his chair and lowered his chin.

"Oh, yes, I am. But we'll get to what I need in return in a few minutes." Lincoln shifted his stance as he collected his thoughts. "What's your problem with Stormi?"

"We need her to back off," Dante said. "Not only is it imperative she not find out I'm alive, but her continuing to hack into the system will put everyone who had a hand in blowing up that rocket ship on high alert."

"They are already running scared since she leaked documents and now the current launch is on hold." Jimmy waved his hand over the computer. "My plan is contingent on Zero Gravity moving forward."

Lincoln pinched the bridge of his nose. "Does that mean you have proof they sabotaged the first launch and tried to kill Dante in the first place?"

"We don't have all the evidence, but we're close and perhaps you can help us find it with your new security system." Jimmy batted his eyelashes like a sexy little vixen.

Lincoln laughed. "I guess I walked right into giving you what you wanted in the first place."

"I just need to be able to find the proof and it's somewhere in those digital hallways," Jimmy said.

"No offense, but I also had a little chat with Darius and Fenmore about you, and while you have some skills, you don't have the computer savvy to do what you need to. You won't find it. Not without my help. So, why don't you let me do it. I'm in there anywhere. David just gave me access to everything, finally."

"He probably deleted shit if he made you wait," Dante muttered.

"If he did, I'll be able to see that. I might not know exactly what was there, but there will be a trace left behind, which means I'll be able to dig." Lincoln nodded. "I might not be the great Darius Ford, but I am the next best thing." He lifted his finger. "Once you have your proof, what's your next move?"

"We shut down Zero Gravity and arrest David, his daughter, and anyone else who was involved in the explosion and the cover-up," Jimmy said.

"What about Dante's work?" Lincoln asked, although this was more for Stormi than for himself. "I understand that you most likely did not sabotage those rocket boosters, but according to the reports, the work you did on them was suspect and subpar."

"Not true," Dante said behind a tight jaw. "We believe David stole my designs and will be using them on this next launch. But we need to find them to prove it."

"That makes sense." Lincoln should be able to find them easily enough.

"So, will you be able to keep Stormi out of the system?" Jimmy stood, resting his ass on the desk. "And what are your demands?"

Oh boy. Neither of these men were going to like what he had in mind. "They aren't demands and the first one only came to light after speaking with you." Lincoln pointed to the computer. "I want you to leave Norman out of this. Release him. We don't need his credentials. He'll end up collateral damage and his boy is on his way to the Air Force Academy. I'd hate for anything to taint that young man's record before it even begins."

"Norman's not going to like it. He wants to take them down. His wife has done nothing but fuck with his kid's life," Dante said.

"Tell him whatever you have to, including letting him know I'm in on this plan if that's what it will take," Lincoln said. "But I want him and his son protected. Deal?"

"I'll make it happen." Jimmy nodded. "What else?"

"I need help figuring out if my boss and ex-girlfriend has anything to do with why I'm here. As in, if she's setting me up to fail," Lincoln said.

"Are you fucking kidding me? If that's the case, you should be letting me inside that system with you." Jimmy glared.

"No. Because she'll know you're there. She's as good as I am. In some ways, better. Not at the coding, but because she's a lying bitch." Lincoln held up his hand. "What I need you to do is use your knowledge of this case and all your contacts to figure out if she's working with David, Jeannie, or anyone else inside Zero Gravity. I can't do it because it's possible she's inside the system watching me, and because she's my boss, she'll have access to the new code, but I'm working on a solution to that, once I find her spying on me."

"This is giving me one hell of a headache," Dante whispered. "Who is this woman and what's the name of the company?"

"This is where it gets interesting. Her name is Samantha Wilkerson. She owns CyberGuard Solutions. I just learned that Samantha worked for the company that installed the current system and was on the original team that created the system." Lincoln waved his hand. "According to my ex, David is not aware of this, but something tells me that's not true. But for Samantha, this is her chance to save face because she's taking this personally."

"She worked for Ironclad Security? They are a British firm." Dante rubbed his chin. "I think I remember when their team toured Zero Gravity."

"Does this woman look familiar to you?" Lincoln had never been so happy to have not deleted something from his phone. He held up an old image of Samantha.

"It's been a long time." Dante leaned closer. "I can't be sure, but the name does sound familiar and so does her face. My team submitted parameters for the scope of our work and the kind of computer system we needed. I might be able to dig up the emails."

"That would be helpful." Lincoln nodded. "Now, for my last request and this is the only way I can keep an eye on what Stormi is doing."

"Like hell." Dante lunged forward. "You are not using my daughter."

Lincoln blew out a puff of air. "Look. It's either I chase her in and out of their system, wasting precious time, because she's determined to clear your name. Or I use her skills to help me figure all this out, all while clearing your name."

"He's got a point," Jimmy said. "This way we control the narrative."

"I don't like it." Dante shook his head.

"Can't say it's my first choice." Lincoln smiled

weakly. “But this way, I can protect her identity as well as keep you dead to her for a little while longer.” He turned his attention toward Jimmy. “You think you can help me with my Samantha problem?”

“Already on it.”

“All right.” Lincoln waved his cell. “I’ll send you a secure number you can reach me on. Don’t leave a message if I don’t answer. I’ll see that you called.” He pointed to Jimmy’s computer. “I take it that’s always secure.”

“It is.”

“Okay. We can message on that. I’ll be in touch tonight after I’ve had a fun little chat with Stormi. Let’s hope she doesn’t beat me over the head with a baseball bat.” Lincoln gripped the handle and swallowed. It was one thing to come clean about one betrayal, but to layer on a different one?

Yeah, he was going to hell.

CHAPTER TEN

Stormi hugged her notebooks to her chest as she walked up the pathway to her front door, mentally tossing daggers at Lincoln. She had a couple of reasons to be pissed off, but only two that she could share, and they didn't warrant this level of anger. Not even considering they'd slept together.

They weren't a couple. Actually, they were perfect strangers who agreed whatever was brewing between them was nothing more than a fling.

They had the hots for each other and it was one way to deal with the sexual tension.

The only problem with that was they were both hiding a secret. Hers was a massive one and it was twofold.

And they'd both caught each other in a web of lies.

That was the irony of the whole fucked-up situation. She knew he'd been in her system but couldn't say one fucking word about it.

Neither could he.

And now, if she was going to clear her father's name, she had to come up with a plan B.

She sucked in a deep breath and collected her thoughts.

Lincoln sat in one of the cheap folding chairs she'd picked up at a garage sale when she'd first blown into town. There had been three places for rent that she could afford.

This one. A one-bedroom apartment, and a house twenty minutes away that was a little too close to a community where many employees of Zero Gravity lived. While she wanted access, she didn't want to live among them.

The one-bedroom was out of the question. There was no way to hide her equipment under lock and key. She needed at least two, but nothing had been available for a short-term rental, and she hadn't planned on staying too long. She'd hoped she'd be able to be in and out under three months.

It appeared it might take longer than that.

"Good evening." Lincoln set his laptop aside and smiled as if everything was right and good in the world. "How was work?"

"Fine." She cocked her head. "Though I'm a little annoyed with you. I expected to see you at the library today." She waved her notebook. "I did all this work for you and you couldn't be bothered to call or respond to my texts. And now you have the nerve to sit here on my front porch and assume I want to spend time with you?"

"I appreciate all you are doing." He rose. "I'm sorry. I should have texted as soon as I got here and asked if it was okay to wait. I haven't been in town all day. My breakfast meeting lasted through lunch, and then I chased down some intel."

"It would have taken you all of one minute to shoot me a message. I was honestly worried about you." That wasn't a lie. Although, she was more concerned about what he might be finding out about her and her true identity. All day, the nagging question as to why he suspected anything about her and her secret room twisted around in her brain like a snake coiling, preparing to strike. Had he come here knowing all along who she was?

That thought made her sick to her stomach because it meant sleeping with her was simply part of his master plan and had nothing to do with being attracted to her at all.

He leaned over and lifted a bag. "I got a couple of nice bottles of wine. Can we go inside and I'll pour us each a glass? I took the liberty of ordering food from Zeke's place. It will be here within the hour."

"That's pretty presumptuous of you to believe that I would forgive you that easily."

"Besides wanting to discuss the research that you did, I'd like to tell you some of things I learned today."

"That better be some good wine." She waved her finger. "And I hope you ordered me a nice fat juicy steak with their garlic mashed potatoes and asparagus, or I'll really be pissed."

He chuckled. "Looks like I nailed it." He waved his hand toward the door. "After you." He bent over and gathered his belongings.

"For the record, I'm only mad that you ignored me after asking me to do you a favor. I don't want you believing I'm some needy chick or anything." As she strolled down the hallway past her office, she noticed it wasn't locked. Her heart lurched to the back of her throat. She tried to swallow, but her muscles didn't work properly.

Kurt had always told her she had a shitty poker face because she didn't spend enough time around people. Working at bookstores and now the library, she'd developed a more natural state of fakeness.

But she still sucked at lying outside of her new identity, but she didn't view that as anything other than survival. While Kurt wasn't coming after her, the men he helped to launder money might. Though Kara did mention those men could be facing real prison time for other crimes.

That would certainly make her feel a lot better.

"I would never think that about you." He set his

computer on the counter. "And it's nice to have someone care." He kissed her cheek.

"I wouldn't go that far. But I'd hate for you to wrap Tal's Jeep around a telephone pole."

"Ouch." He laughed as he took the corkscrew to the bottle.

She pulled two glasses from cupboard and checked them to make sure they were clean. It was rare that she used anything other than paper plates and red Solo cups. As wasteful as that was, she was too lazy these days to do anything else. Besides, she often ordered out, and those came in perfectly good containers that she could eat from.

"Come on. Let's sit out back. It's a nice night," Lincoln said.

"I don't have anything in the backyard to sit on." She lifted the glass and took a sip. Damn, that was good. She kept her gaze on the red liquid and away from Lincoln's scrutinizing gaze. Something definitely had his panties in a twist. While she wanted to know, she didn't feel like dealing with this delicate dance they'd begun.

He tucked his laptop under his arm. "I picked up a couple of Adirondack chairs in my travels, so you do now." He wrangled the sliding doors, which she wondered if they were going to fall out of their tracks every time she opened them.

"And how much did those cost? Because I'm on a budget."

"They're plastic, so not very much. I bought a bunch for my patio and picked up two extra for yours. Consider it a gift."

"Thank you," she managed behind a tight jaw. "But please don't do anything like that again."

"If you really want to pay me back, they were thirty dollars apiece." He eased into one of them and set his computer on the table. "The table was forty, I believe." He stretched out his legs, crossed his ankles, and tilted his head toward the sky. "I need you to let me talk. It's going to be hard for you to keep quiet. You're going to get mad. Scared. All sorts of things. But I'm begging you to let me get through everything I have to say before you open your mouth."

"Not sure I can do that, but I'll try."

"I appreciate the honesty," he said. "I started my day with more than conflicting emotions." He laughed. "I had every intention of keeping you in the dark. Of controlling the situation. Of manipulating you by manipulating your system."

"You had no right to—"

"That's not the point." He reached over and pressed his finger over her lips. "I got one hell of a good chuckle when you stopped me dead in my tracks for half a minute. The popup was funny. I loved the reference. That might have scared someone else off, but you failed to account for the fact that I know who you are… Amanda." He lowered his chin and arched a brow.

"I have no idea what you're talking about."

"I'll let you have your lie for now." He raised his glass, swirled the wine, and then brought it to his lips and took a long swig. "I believed that if I could watch what you were doing, while I dealt with some things that weren't adding up, I could isolate the issue and keep you from doing something stupid. However, as today progressed, and I learned some things that I plan on filling you in on, I realized that the two of us working together would be better."

"I've already agreed to help you with research. I'm not sure what else I can do for you."

"Really? You're going to keep this up?" He jerked his thumb over his shoulder. "I know you saw that your office was unlocked. We both know it was you I saw in the digital hallways in Zero Gravity and that it was me who hacked your computer system this morning." He leaned closer. "Not only are you Amanda Norris, but you're also the ethical hacker known as Twister. I'd know her work anywhere. I'm quite impressed." He pressed his mouth over hers in a soft, but tender kiss. "And before you go and deny it again, I've got sources with the FBI. I've confirmed it. And your secret is more than safe with me. I also want to help you. Something very wonky is going on with Zero Gravity. My boss—"

"You mean your ex-girlfriend."

"Semantics, but yes, her." Lincoln nodded. "I want to help you find the proof you need to exonerate your father's name because I believe he's innocent. But I need your help because I think Samantha is setting me up."

"For what?" She wiggled her finger. "And I'm not admitting to anything or agreeing to help. I just want more information."

"That's fair." He set his wine on the patio table and opened his laptop. "There are a couple of things that Samantha didn't tell me when I took this job. She sort of owned up to one, but she is still keeping certain information from me about it." He tapped the keyboard. "To make a very long story short, she wrote the original security program for Zero Gravity."

"Why didn't she go in and immediately patch it when I breached the system?"

Lincoln smiled and winked at her admission.

She poked his arm. "Just answer the question."

"Because they chose a new company. Her company. And she wanted to save face."

"She didn't want David to know it was her system that got breached out of fear he would fire her ass."

"Something like that." Lincoln nodded. "But I think that's only one small piece of what's really going on. Here. Look at this." He handed her his computer.

She set her wine aside and scanned the code. Her pulse raced. Her palms grew sweaty. "Where did you get this?"

"Three years ago, while I was still with the Special Boat Service, Samantha asked me to take a look at that. I was already familiar with your work as Twister because of Operation Turncoat, but Samantha couldn't have known that."

"I'm sorry, I've honestly never heard of that."

"A digital bank heist involving international terrorists. My government worked with yours to take down this ring. You were hired as a consultant by the bank after their system was hacked."

"Okay, that part I remember. Kurt was a little butthurt they only wanted me, but the president of the bank was someone my father knew." She turned her gaze. "Why does your ex-girlfriend have the code that landed me in prison?" Stormi saw no point in lying anymore.

"I don't know," Lincoln said. "When she showed this to me three years ago, it was all about finding out who the second coder was."

"That's easy, it was Kurt. He fucked with my code, making it look like I was the one helping those thugs. But again, why would someone across the pond care? The only people this affected were the companies Kurt was helping and using me to do it."

"When she asked me to look at it, I was deployed more than I was home. I wasn't working with her or doing any contract work for her company. But she did occasionally ask for my advice and opinions." He tapped the screen. "In this case, she wanted to see how quickly I could detect the odd lines of code."

Stormi turned her attention back to the computer

screen. She highlighted the lines of code that weren't her own. "This isn't right."

"What do you mean?"

"These aren't the lines of code that got me arrested. They're different. Not as close to my own. What Kurt did was better. He mimicked mine so tightly that on its first run, I missed it."

"When did you catch it?"

"I always do a second run. He kept trying to distract me and offering to do it for me. He also stated that the customer was happy and it worked fine, so I should leave well enough alone. But I'm a perfectionist. So I couldn't. That's when I caught it. I confronted him. I told him I was going to turn him in, but it was too late. The Feds were already knocking down my door."

"They arrested you. Not him, right?"

She nodded. "It was my code. My client. It wasn't until Special Agent Kara Martin got me alone and listened to me. Really listened to me." Stormi narrowed her stare. "Have you looked into how your ex and my ex might have known each other?"

"Personally, I can't do that." He held up his hand. "But I've called in a couple of favors from friends in high places. However, we have to be careful. We can't tip our hand."

"Are we seriously going down a conspiracy theory rabbit hole?" she asked.

"I did a scan of Zero Gravity's system today. Not the entire system, just where the breach took place.

You left a breadcrumb where you got in. It wasn't easy to find and when I did locate it, I moved past it quickly and zoomed in on something else. But if I found that line, then Samantha could find it too. And the thing is, I can't trust that she's not watching me." He pursed his lips. "I'm afraid to scan my system in fear she'll catch me catching her."

"What's the likelihood she's in mine?"

"Since I hacked yours this morning, it's possible."

"Fuck," Stormi mumbled.

"A buddy of mine who works for a very prestigious organization is setting me up with a state-of-the-art computer system. It will arrive tomorrow. It will be free of any possible malware or spyware. You can begin infiltrating both your systems with that tomorrow while I continue to do my job."

"You want me to spy on you?"

"I want you to do more than that." He nodded, leaning closer, taking her chin with his thumb and forefinger. "I want you to find the evidence that links Samantha to Kurt. That proves she weakened their system so you could get in, find a few documents, leak them, and sabotage Zero Gravity so she could get the contract."

"And why would she do that?"

"To do the same thing Kurt did to you. Destroy me. In the process, she'll destroy you as well."

"I don't know. All the dots aren't connecting for me." Stormi closed the computer and snagged her wine, taking a big gulp. "Jeannie came to the library today. At first, I thought she might be there checking up on her son, but she didn't even know he was there and couldn't have cared less."

"What did she want?"

"She took out one of the books I was looking at for research. I thought it was strange. Don't you? Especially when she said my library was the only one that had it, which wasn't true. Zero Gravity has its own library and they have three copies."

"Did Kurt ever spend any time overseas?"

"He did a semester abroad and after he graduated, he worked for an international company for six months," Stormi said. "He fell in love with Europe then and he'd go back once a year. I never went with him. I'm not a huge fan of traveling, and it was always a boys' trip for him, though he did tell me he dated someone for a few months, but it didn't work out which is why he came home. We'd been corresponding and I wanted to start my own company, and so did he." She pushed to a standing position and stared at the setting sun. Her mind rolled to the past. She rubbed her wrist as the memory of metal tightening on her skin tickled her brain. "How old is Samantha?"

"Thirty-four. Why?"

"Kurt's thirty-three." She turned. "Did she ever work at a company called Secure Technologies?"

"She did," Lincoln said. "It didn't last more than a year, I believe. It was long before me, but it was after that gig that she went to work for Ironclad Securities, which is the company—"

"That did the original system for Zero Gravity." Stormi turned and planted her hands on her hips. "So, your ex and my ex were something of an item back in the day. That means, Samantha must suspect I'm alive, which means Kurt must think that too." She fiddled with a few stray locks of hair. "Who else knows I'm alive? And who in your circle, or mine, have you spoken to about this?"

"Tal knows, but Heather does not. Outside of that, I haven't told anyone. I have spoken to Kara." He closed the gap, covering her mouth, silencing her, which pissed her off. "I haven't told her everything and I don't think we should because I don't want her swooping in and relocating you. I can protect you. Besides, I do want to help you find the documentation you need to prove your father didn't sabotage those rocket boosters."

She smacked his arm away. "Why would you want to do that? Have you seen something that I haven't? Know something that I don't?"

"I trust my gut and that's telling me everything about this case stinks." He cupped her chin. "And for some godforsaken reason, I trust you. I shouldn't. But I do. Therefore, I believe you."

"Gee, that makes me feel all warm and fuzzy inside."

He chuckled. "So, are we partners?"

"That depends. Have you told me everything?"

"No," he said. "And there are a couple of things I can't tell you. Not because I want to keep them from you, but because the FBI has told me I have to."

"Kara?" Stormi jerked her head back.

"Someone higher up than her." Lincoln wrapped his arms around her waist and brushed his mouth over her lips. "And before you go asking a million more questions that I can't answer at this time, I will fill you in as time goes on when it's appropriate, even if I'm told not to by Kara and her higher-up."

"Are you telling me that to shut me up, or do you mean it?"

"We both have something at stake here. Perhaps you more than me." He thumbed her cheek. "I also find myself doing the one thing I swore I wouldn't do."

"What's that?"

"Care about you." He kissed her nose. "So, yeah. I mean it."

She stared into his eyes, hoping to see the lies behind the words, but all she saw was a man with a deep soul and a trusting heart. She should pack up her things in the middle of the night and disappear.

But she wouldn't.

In his arms, in that moment, she knew she'd found an ally like she'd never known before.

"So, what do we do now?" she asked.

"Once our food gets here, we go back to my place. Your bed sucks."

"I'm offended."

"My back is offended." He laughed. "Tonight we create a plan. Once the equipment arrives from Darius, we go to work."

"I haven't done any real hacking except for Zero Gravity in three years."

"Oh, you forget, I've chatted with Kara. I know—"

"Okay, three jobs." She gripped his shoulders, digging her nails into his thick muscles. "But this is different. There isn't going to be anything holding me back. I can be me again."

He cupped her face. "You're going to have to be disciplined. More so than ever before. If Samantha knows who you are and knows you were the one I collided with in Zero Gravity, she's going to be gunning for you, and she's going to use me to do it. We're going to have to be on our A game if we're going to shut her down and clear your dad."

"Oh, I'm ready."

"That's my girl."

For the first time since she learned of her father's death, Stormi believed she had half a chance of making sure his legacy lived on.

CHAPTER ELEVEN

Lincoln arched, stretching out his back. His muscles ached. His brain hurt. For the last three days, he'd worked tirelessly on the new security system for Zero Gravity. He tweaked and tested and tweaked and tested some more. It wasn't done. Far from it and his frustration came out of the fact that he should be, but because David, and Samantha, chose to keep certain aspects of the original system from him, his code was weak and open to blind spots.

Unfortunately, they were apparent—too obvious—and he needed to correct them if his plan would work.

Lincoln couldn't shake off his doubts about the accuracy of his theory. They hadn't yet tested it under real conditions.

"Lincoln?" Stormi's sweet voice rang out, calming his nerves.

"In my office," he called. He hated admitting how

much he missed her during the daylight hours. Or how her warm body at night affected his heart and soul. Whenever he stared deep into her eyes, it was as if she could see his darkest secrets. His inner fears.

His feelings for her grew too thick, too fast. He was lost in a sea of emotion with no life raft in sight. He drifted off to sleep every night with her in his arms and woke with her body draped over his. It was like nothing he'd ever experienced before, and he'd lived with Samantha.

Only sleeping with her sometimes was like being stuffed inside an icebox next to a couple of lifeless fish, and he wasn't talking about the sex. That wasn't bad. It was actually pretty good when they had it. But outside of that, Samantha was about as cold of a woman as anyone could possibly be.

Stormi, on the other hand, was flesh and blood. She was wild and hot and made his heart beat out of control.

"I brought sustenance." She appeared at the doorway holding a take-out bag from the Sunny Side Up Diner. "I got you a patty melt, onion rings, and a chocolate shake."

"My God, woman. I could kiss you right now."

"I wouldn't say no to that."

He pushed his chair back, stood, took the bag, set it on the desk, and yanked her to his chest, crushing his mouth to hers, melding their lips together like two ships. She tasted like a fine wine and all he wanted to do was get drunk on her rich flavor. "How was work today?"

"Pretty boring." She clasped her fingers behind his neck. "How was your day? Solve your coding problem?"

"What I could with the information I have," he said. "I had a nice little conference call with David and Samantha and according to David, I have everything and when I compare the original system to what I'm working on, it would appear that I do."

"What are you seeing that makes you believe that you don't?"

"Code that was either written by someone other than Samantha, or new code written by Samantha." He leaned against his desk. "Are you ready to do a little fishing?"

She arched a brow. "Are you serious?"

He nodded. "I told Samantha someone tried to break through my firewall today, but I shut it down. However, I also told her that I put a crack in the system and that the hacker tagged it. All I have to do is open it and you should come running."

"Does this mean I get to play?" She smiled wide.

"I wasn't about to have all the fun. Besides, while you go in, and my program chases you around, I can do some real digging."

She scowled.

He kissed her nose. "Aw, come on, babe. We both know that Samantha is going to be watching. I need you to lead her down one hallway, while you direct me elsewhere."

"I know. I get that I'm going to be sitting right next to you while you go hunting for intel to clear my dad's name, but sometimes the hacking is half the fun."

He kissed her temple. "I get it. I do. But we have to play this smart. It's not just about your dad, the explosion, and the cover-up. We need to figure out exactly what Samantha has planned for me. If it's a takedown, like Kurt tried to do with you, or if it's something else. Because honestly, it doesn't make sense. You and Kurt had a history of butting heads in your business and he wanted you out so he could go down the path of darkness. For the life of me, I can't figure out—"

"Do you not understand a woman scorned?"

"I didn't scorn Samantha. I'm not the one who cheated." Lincoln arched a brow. "I invested in her company. Literally gave her all the money I had, and what do I have to show for it? Fucking nothing. I'm the one who has something to be bitter about." He let out a long breath. "Okay. Yeah. I get it. If this job gets fucked up, she doesn't have to pay me and it's also cause to terminate my contract early. It's just one way for her to get rid of me without dealing with me." He took Stormi's chin with his palm. "But she knows me pretty well and knows that while I don't give a shit about money and might be willing to part with that just to be done with her, I would fight her tooth and nail if it meant my integrity. I was a poor boy from the streets. I once had to fight, steal, and beg for food. I worked damn hard to get where I am and wouldn't let her, or anyone else for that matter, strip me of what I've bled for without a fight."

"Is it bad that I'm totally turned on right now?"

Lincoln shook his head as he ran his hand under her shirt, fingering the hook of her bra. "We have time and I would never dare deprive you of your wants, needs, or desires."

"I would hope not." Stormi tore his shirt over his head and tossed it to the floor before shoving him back to his chair. It rolled into the desk with a resounding thud. Leaning over him, she kissed her way down his chest and stomach while working on the button and zipper to his jeans.

"What do you think you're doing?"

She shimmied out of her blouse and bra, smiling up at him as she settled between his legs, taking him into her hands, and gently stroking his length. "Having my way with you."

He swallowed hard; his throat suddenly dry. "And if I told you to stop?"

Her smile widened, dark and seductive. "Would you really want me to?" They both knew the answer to that question. In the short time he'd known Stormi, she'd always been bold, dominant even, but in moments like these, Lincoln could only marvel at her confidence and poise. She was the sun wrapped in the bright-blue sky with a fiery passion burning beneath her touch.

"I thought so," she murmured as she continued her exploration. Her fingers set every nerve on fire. He gripped the armrests of his chair tightly, biting back a moan.

Her brazen actions were making him lose control and he loved every second of it. He watched her, his breath hot and heavy as she moved her hands confidently over him.

Stormi rose to her feet and dropped her slacks to the floor. She straddled him in the chair. Her eyes held a certain level of satisfaction as she saw the effect she had over his mind, body, and soul.

With a smirk that promised everything yet nothing at all, she leaned down slowly until their lips were just a breath away from each other's.

"Let's have some fun," she whispered with a wicked glint in her eyes before sealing their fate with a searing kiss.

His hands, trembling from the anticipation, sought out the faint curve of her hips. He drew her closer, their bodies fitting together like two pieces of a long-lost puzzle. Each touch from her was a scorching brand against his skin. The taste of her lips as she claimed him with a fervor that matched his own, the feel of her pressed against him, was intoxicating.

She pulled back abruptly, leaving him panting and yearning for more. Her eyes were full of mischievous sparks as she reached behind to unclip her bra. It fell to the floor forgotten, a casualty in this game of desire they were playing.

"Stormi..." His voice came out hoarse and pleading.

Her fingers danced along his chest, tracing invisible patterns that left him shivering with want. "Shh..." She silenced him with a finger against his lips, replacing it seconds later with another heady kiss.

Her hands gripped his shoulders as she began to move against him in a rhythm that made his world tilt on its axis. His hands roamed freely through the expanse of soft skin on display before him, setting ablaze every inch he touched.

He was lost to the sensations she was stirring within him. His senses were filled with Stormi—her touch, her scent, her taste. Her name escaped his lips in delirious pleas as she continued to push him closer and closer to the edge.

With one last coy smile, she pressed herself harder against him, driving Lincoln to utter surrender wrapped in boundless ecstasy.

As they collapsed into each other's arms, spent and contented from their ballet of passion and desire, Lincoln knew he wouldn't trade this moment or any other with Stormi for anything else. As he held her close, listening to the rhythmic lullaby of her heartbeat under his ear, he realized that he was irrevocably lost in her, and he wouldn't have it any other way.

"You're incredible," he whispered. "I'm addicted to you."

"That's a sweet thing to say."

He cupped her face and stared intently into her eyes, searching them for a reason to say something bullish. To push her away and make her hate him in this moment, because as soon as she found out that he was keeping from her the one thing that mattered to her more than anything, she'd never speak to him again anyway. "I told myself this could be a fling. That I wouldn't fall for you. But I'm falling so hard it hurts." His heart rattled around in his throat like a drunken sailor, unable to stand up straight. His breath hitched.

"You're serious, aren't you?" She bit down on her lower lip and let out an audible gasp.

"I didn't mean to freak you out or come on too strong. But you have to know that I would have played my cards very differently if I didn't care about you."

She dropped her head to his shoulder, nuzzling her face in his neck. "You are playing a little bit with fire by helping me."

"Not a little bit. A lot." He lifted her chin. "The moment I learned of who you were, I should have stopped talking to you. I certainly shouldn't have brought you into my circle and asked for help. I should have shut you down and blocked you from the system. But I couldn't do that. And not just because I wanted and needed your help. You have to know that I truly want to see your father vindicated."

"I do believe you." She kissed his cheek. "This is going to come out backward because I didn't want to have feelings for you, but I do and that scares the crap out of me."

"Trust me. I understand." He patted her bottom. "Now, let's get dressed. Eat our food. And get to work. It could prove to be a long night." What he really needed was a phone call to Jimmy because he couldn't keep fucking lying to her this way.

CHAPTER TWELVE

"Why hasn't anyone taken the bait?" Stormi handed Lincoln a mug of coffee and leaned against the kitchen counter. It had been a week since she'd entered the digital hallway, and Lincoln gave her forty minutes before he chased her out. He was nearly done with the new system. It would be implemented in the next few days. Once that was done, it would be much harder for them to lurk in the shadows.

But what really got under her skin was that they couldn't find Samantha in Lincoln's system, but she could feel her presence like an alligator hiding beneath the murky water's surface, waiting to take its prey in its powerful jaws.

Lincoln took his coffee and sipped. He had dark circles under his eyes. He'd barely slept in days between writing code during daylight hours and setting traps in the evening. He threaded his fingers through his wet hair. "I've got a call with Samantha in twenty minutes. Care to listen in?"

"I'd love to." She glanced at her watch. "But I have to be at the library in an hour."

"I'll make sure I send you notes as soon as I'm done with her. She wants an update on the system and where I'm at with you."

"You mean the hacker."

He chuckled. "Exactly."

"Only we both know she can see me along with someone else. Any idea on who that is?"

"It could be Tony, the guy I caught her fucking on my desk when we were still together. He used to be someone I called a friend," Lincoln said. "Last I heard, they weren't an item, but I always believed they only pretended to call it off while she tried to get me back."

"Why continue with the farse after you decided to move to the States?"

Lincoln shrugged. "It could have been Tony's idea. He's reached out a few times, apologizing, stating that Samantha told him we had broken up. But I know that's bullshit." Lincoln set his mug to the side. "We're missing something."

"Yeah, and the investigation into Zero Gravity is coming up empty. Kara told me that they may be given the go-ahead to launch in two weeks."

"Which coincides with my upload to the new security system." He pinched the bridge of my nose. "I smell a setup of epic proportions. But I can't find her anywhere."

"I bet she won't show up with whatever she plans on doing to your coding until after the final test."

"That means she's taking my coding as I do it." He folded his arms.

"She's got to know I'm alive. But how could she know I'm here in Fallport, working with you?"

"Any number of ways. It's not like we've kept ourselves hidden," Lincoln said. "People in this town have seen us together. Most assume we're dating. She also knows my type, and you pretty much fit that bill."

"I don't appreciate being boiled down to a cookie-cutter role of a female."

He cocked his head. "I didn't mean it that way. But before I dated Samantha, I was involved with an MI6 agent. She was in the cybercrimes unit. That's what I meant by a type."

"Even so, I've only been here now going on three months."

"All right, but let's look at this logically. Samantha didn't assign me this job until after you hacked into Zero Gravity. That was after you moved here and while it was my idea for this being my final rodeo, she didn't fight me on it. As a matter of fact, now that I think about it, she led me down that train of thought."

"What was your plan of action before you took this job?"

"Long story short, I had negotiated myself down

from a five-year contract to two years. I was going to suffer through that, until this landed in my lap, bringing me here." He tapped his temple. "She knew Tal was here. It was Heather who set us up."

"How did Samantha and Heather know each other?"

"They didn't. Not really. They randomly met at a coffee shop when Tal and Heather were visiting. This was before you were arrested, while you were still living in Saratoga and starting your company with Kurt… well, shit. How did you and Kurt get your funding?"

"Same way everyone else does these days. We had investors."

"Any of them anonymous? Or LLCs out of the UK?"

"Could be," she said. "Kurt handled most of that."

"We need to dig up your company's financials as well as Samantha's. I bet we find a connection." He shook his head. "Jesus. I can't believe I didn't think of this sooner. But I would wager that some of this, at least from Samantha's perspective, has to do with making sure that I somehow out you as Amanda, while fucking up so badly that we both end up in prison and Kurt gets out. But I know something that they don't." He blew out a puff of air. "I need to make a few phone calls before I chat with Samantha and I'm going to need some privacy for that."

"I thought we didn't keep secrets from each other anymore."

He cupped her face. "Remember when I told you

there were a few things I wasn't telling you? Well, this is one of them and before I do tell you, I need to handle something first."

"Am I going to be pissed off?"

"You're going to hate me," he mumbled. "But if by doing so, it's kept you both safe, then I'll live with that."

"Both?"

"I need you to trust me." He kissed her lips. It was kind. Warm. Loving.

"How can I do that when you won't tell me everything?"

"Because outside of when I hacked your system, I haven't lied to you about anything, except this, and I've only done so because I've had to. Hopefully, you'll understand and forgive me." He rested his forehead against hers. "I promise, we'll talk about this tonight and I'll tell you what I can."

"Why can't I know now?"

"Babe." He closed his eyes. "I shouldn't have said anything to begin with, but keeping this from you has been eating me alive. Whatever this is between us came on so fast, my head is spinning. I don't want to ruin it. But I have a job to do and part of that includes protecting you."

"Lying to me doesn't protect me." Her heart dropped to her big toe. Not only had she put her trust in Lincoln, but she'd put her father's legacy in his hands. All her hard work, she'd handed over to Lincoln on a silver platter. She'd given him everything she'd learned. She walked him through the digital files where she believed her father's research had been stored. Together, they'd found nothing. But what if he'd found something while she'd been holed up at the library and he chose not to share it with her?

"It's not like I lied to you because I wanted to. I had to." He blinked.

"No. You chose to and without knowing what it is you're keeping from me, I don't know how to process anything going forward."

He brushed her hair over her shoulder. "I will send you everything I can on Samantha's financials. Will you try to make that connection for me today? Please? We'll talk tonight about everything else. Promise."

"All right."

"That's my girl." He kissed her nose. "Be safe."

"You too." Only she had started to wonder if she was safe in his presence anymore.

LINCOLN POUNDED his fist against the motel door a little more aggressively than necessary. However, his emotions had a death grip on his heart. This case wasn't just about him and ridding himself of his past. That may have been what he thought it had been all about, but Samantha had played him. She had to have known. That was the only thing that made sense, especially since she had ties to Kurt.

The question that weighed heavily on his mind now was if Jimmy knew.

Now that would really fucking piss him off.

The door rattled. "What the fuck?" Jimmy stared at him with wide eyes. "Get inside." He peeked his head outside before slamming the door shut. "Did anyone follow you?"

"No," Lincoln said.

"Is my little girl okay?" Dante jumped up from the bed. "Did something happen?"

"Oh, a lot has happened and I need answers, starting with, did either of you know that my boss knew her husband?" He glared at Jimmy. His stomach twisted in one hell of knot. "And don't bullshit me because if what I believe is happening, my freedom is hanging in the balance."

Jimmy turned and made his way to the small desk in front of the window. He sat down and leaned back. "What exactly have you learned?"

"You don't get to answer with a question," Lincoln said. "I don't appreciate being used as a pawn. Especially not when I'm the one helping you." He cocked his head. "Start talking, and then maybe I'll tell you what I know."

"Sounds like you know more than we do," Dante said.

"I'm not so sure about that." Lincoln let out a long breath and eased onto the corner of the bed. "So, you both already knew Samantha and Kurt had a connection."

"I didn't know shit until this man plucked me from the rehab center where my identity was being withheld from the world. I didn't even know the government had faked my death." Dante held Lincoln's gaze.

"Be quiet, Dante," Jimmy said in a low growl. "Lincoln knows how this works. The left hand often doesn't talk to the right. He's gone on missions where he knows he's only been given half the intel."

"And I've always hated that." Lincoln shook his head. "If you've read anything about me, you'd know that I've broken ranks more than once because of that. I don't like to see good men die because we either don't have all the information, or we've been given misinformation all in the name of protecting the integrity of something greater than what we were sent to do." He rubbed his temples. "Samantha is doing her fucking best to make sure I go down for something. I'm not exactly sure what her end game is. It could be running on the assumption that Stormi will be able to breach my system and Samantha will give her access to something she thinks she can use to leak to the press, making me look bad."

"But that makes her and her company appear incompetent," Jimmy said. "Yeah, I knew about her connection to Kurt." He turned and tapped his fingers on the keyboard. "Look."

Lincoln rose and strolled across the room.

"We found images of Kurt and Samantha together when he studied abroad. And again when he took trips to Europe." Jimmy tapped the screen. "He was even seen with her when the two of you were together."

"Jesus," Lincoln muttered.

"We have a paper trail that proves Samantha invested in Kurt's company and that they collaborated together on a few jobs." Jimmy glanced up. "Including the ones that got Stormi arrested."

"You've got to be fucking kidding me. Why?" Lincoln planted his hands on his hips. "Outside of jealousy."

"Why do you say that?" Dante asked.

"Because Samantha showed me code that was written by your daughter years ago, and I could see in her eyes how jealous she was of Stormi's brilliance. Hell, I was impressed. But Samantha, as smart as she is, doesn't like to play second fiddle."

"One thing I do know about my daughter is that she always stressed the ethics when she talked to me about her job," Dante said. "Because it was such a bone of contention with me. Not just because I didn't understand it, but because I thought Kurt was such a slime."

"Did Stormi ever mention anything about Kurt asking her to do anything that could be considered unethical?" Jimmy asked.

Lincoln blew out a puff of air. "No. It all came down to him changing her coding. But both you and Kara are the ones who have the evidence she turned over that helped put him away."

Jimmy nodded. "She gave us all the original programs she wrote, which didn't match what was given to us originally when we made the initial arrest. We let her hack into all Kurt's clients as well as the ones she'd taken on while one of our experts watched. That's how we nailed Kurt. But to be honest, the only person at the time who even remotely believed her was Kara. Most of us went into it thinking she was looking for a way out of trouble. Or at least a way to lessen her time in prison. We were willing to go with it if it meant getting Kurt, since we believed the tip came from him." Jimmy held up his finger. "However, we've done a deeper dive, and that tip might have been routed from the UK."

"Fucking Samantha." Lincoln's head hurt. This was such a convoluted scheme it was almost brilliant. But it had so many holes. So many places it could go wrong. "I still don't get the connection with Zero Gravity. Other than Samantha wrote the original code that Stormi breached. And it can't be only that they figured out Stormi was still alive and she was the one who leaked the documents, shutting down the launch, because what difference does that make for Kurt or Samantha?"

"After I thought my daughter died by suicide, I visited Kurt in prison," Dante said. "I loathed that man. I believed he destroyed any chance I had for a reconciliation with my kid. After they got married, I decided I needed to try because I realized he wasn't going away. I'd always thought he'd pushed her into this ethical hacking job, but the more she and I talked, the more I learned that wasn't the case. It was still a struggle, but we were getting closer. However, Kurt was in her ear, telling her that I was judging them. Judging him. That all I ever did was make her feel bad about herself and her life choices. That I'd ripped her from her childhood home and destroyed her dreams." Dante swiped at his cheeks. "Maybe I did do that, but I was trying, and I was giving that asshole a chance, yet he would twist my passion for developing a more energy-efficient rocker booster as being a shitty father who didn't care about her or her dreams. He'd lied to her more than once, saying that I couldn't come visit because my job meant more to me than her. Only, he was the one who told me not to come because she wasn't ready to spend time with me."

Lincoln paced in the small room. "That explosion was blamed on your faulty boosters."

"They weren't faulty. Zero Gravity didn't use them. Well, they did, but they fucked with them, using an older prototype, but I can't prove it. Not yet anyway."

Lincoln paused. "That's what Stormi's been looking for, but she doesn't really know that's the piece of the puzzle. We've been roaming those digital hallways, looking for anything to clear your name. It would have been nice to know that. I could have narrowed the search."

"Come on. It will be hidden in an encrypted file somewhere," Jimmy said. "You've always been looking for a needle in a haystack. But you're right. The real question is, what does Samantha and Kurt have to do with this? We're not exactly sure outside of these four images." Jimmy tapped on the keyboard. "Samantha has been seen with David or his daughter twice in the UK and twice in the States. The first time was eight years ago when David went to Europe. Here they are in a café. It appears to be a heated conversation. It lasted twenty minutes. About a year later, Samantha came to the States. She starts by meeting with Jeannie. David shows up around a half hour later and he looks pissed. Fast-forward to three months before Stormi was arrested. David and Jeannie fly to Europe. They both have a sit-down with Samantha. It's all nicey-nice. A computer is opened. Files are passed around. But it's the last meeting a month later that's really interesting when Kurt shows up."

"Seriously?" Lincoln leaned forward and stared at the image. "Why didn't you fucking tell me all this last week?"

"Because we don't know what it means, exactly. We don't know what stake Samantha has in Zero Gravity or the launch. She has no money invested in the company and if your program fails, she fails. So this doesn't make sense."

"Only, it's all starting to make perfect fucking sense." Lincoln raked his fingers through his hair. "My program isn't going to fail. When Samantha first sent me here, she made a big deal about me finishing the security program. But she knew I wouldn't let go of the idea that someone hacked the system. She knew I'd want to set a trap, or at the very least find the person. Especially, once I learned it was her program to begin with. They needed to know who was poking around inside and who leaked the information. They knew it was directly linked to the rocket launch; therefore, they suspected it was Stormi."

"Kurt did tell me how shocked he was that Stormi hung herself. That he struggled to believe it. He even leaned closer and flat-out laid out a scenario how the FBI cut her a deal and she sent him up the river, when it was her all along," Dante said. "I had to admit, that made me pause. My girl is a lot of things, including one big old introvert with an old soul. But suicidal? Never."

"Jeannie showed up at the library last week. She spoke to Stormi." Lincoln arched a brow. "I've been seen around town with Stormi. Hell, she might as well be living with me. Everyone believes we're a couple, including Jeannie's son. Whatever their plan had been, it's shifted." He pointed toward Dante. "Who at Zero Gravity would be given credit for any new technology when this investigation is over and the launch is rescheduled? Because I would bet they will be using the rocket boosters you invented. The ones that supposedly blew up."

"Everyone on my team died in that explosion," Dante whispered. "A man by the name of Jasper Booking heads up a second team, but I couldn't tell you anything about his boosters or if they were even viable."

"What about Jeannie?" Lincoln asked. "Aren't you the one who said she's smart and has a degree in physics?"

"Yeah, but her father has never wanted her to be a part of the business. He's so old-fashioned. Doesn't believe a woman's place is anywhere but the kitchen," Dante said.

Lincoln pointed to the laptop. "She's got something on her father. Something that has to do with Samantha. Maybe even Samantha and Kurt. We find that, we find whatever is driving this." For the first time in a few days, Lincoln felt as though he had something to go on. A direction that might land them with answers and a way to finish this once and for all. "What's happening to Stormi and me is payback for different things. We're collateral damage in a different game, but whatever game that is, I was needed for that final battle. Now all I have to do is build my Trojan horse and find that one missing piece."

Dante jumped to his feet. "You have to protect my daughter. She can't get hurt in all of this. She's been through enough."

"I won't let anything happen to her. I promise." Lincoln pulled out his cell.

"What are you doing?" Jimmy asked.

"I'm calling a friend of mine with MI6. I have a sinking feeling that Samantha might have crossed the pond." The cell rang twice.

"Hey, Lincoln. How's America treating you?" Victoria asked.

"Other than my ex is still fucking with my life, great," Lincoln said. "I need a favor."

"Of course you do." Victoria laughed. "How can I be of service?"

"I need you to find out where in the world Samantha is."

"Okay. Let me run her name through Interpol and I'll call you if I get a hit."

"Thanks. I owe you."

"You've been owing me for years." The line went dead.

Lincoln turned his attention to Jimmy. "Even if Samantha didn't cross the pond, I don't think you're safe here. Find another place to hide out. Preferably a little farther away."

"I can do that." Jimmy nodded. "But I need to know what your next move is."

"I'm going to finish the program. Early. I'm going to install it, but I'm going to do it without telling Samantha. She's going to be pissed, and that's the point. I want to watch her go in and change my code while

Stormi and I have a little fun messing with her and hopefully find what we're really looking for, because that's what she'll be protecting. It's there somewhere. It doesn't just disappear. I'm also going to hack into David's and Jeannie's home computers." Lincoln smiled as his heart raced wildly through his system. "I need the FBI to back me up on this because it's technically illegal."

"I'll get someone to sign off on it." Jimmy nodded. "But Samantha's not a US citizen. Not a whole lot we can do with her."

"I've got friends in high places with MI6 and other government agencies in the UK. I'll handle her." Lincoln lifted the shade and peered out the window, making sure no one was in sight. "Watch your backs and let Kara know what's happening." He slipped out the door. First stop, the library. He needed Stormi to take the rest of the day off.

He couldn't do this without her.

Hopefully, she wouldn't kill him first.

CHAPTER THIRTEEN

"Your father's alive."

Stormi stared at Lincoln. Her insides shook like an erupting volcano. Her body was hot lava, filled with rage and an uncontrollable urge to punch him in the throat took hold of her fist. She clenched her hand tightly at her side. "Excuse me? How is that possible?" Only, she knew the answer because she wasn't dead. She took a step backward, not out of fear of Lincoln, but out of fear that she might actually hit the man. "How could you keep that from me?"

"I could ramble off a litany of reasons. Some of them my own. Some of them the FBI's. But none of them matter at this point." Lincoln pulled out one of the stools in front of the island in his kitchen. "I understand you're angry."

"You don't understand shit," she mumbled. "How

long have you known? Before or after we slept together?"

"It was after the first time," he admitted.

"What else are you keeping from me?"

"That's it," he said. "Except for my plan to bring down those who tried to kill him and want to put you back in prison."

"Gee, that doesn't really make up for dick." She poked him in the shoulder. "You're a liar and a snake. Why should I trust you now?"

"Because if we fail, I'll most likely end up back in the UK for treason or some such bullshit." He cocked his head. "The clock is ticking. The investigation into your document leak will be over by the end of the day. I have to finish this program by tomorrow and load it into Zero Gravity before Samantha demands to see it. Not to mention I have confirmation that she's in the States and most likely not far from Fallport. The only intel I don't have is what she's got hanging over David's head, if anything. I'm still working on that piece. But something other than you and Kurt brought those two together."

"Not necessarily." Stormi reached for her hair and twisted her fingers through the strands. "We know that Kurt and Samantha had an affair. We also know that Samantha invested in my company."

"With my money." Lincoln shook his head. "And the two of them have been working together, helping businesses launder money in the States and the UK. But

Zero Gravity isn't laundering money. The only illegal activity they have done is blow up the rocket boosters."

"Plus, murdering good people and blaming my father for it." Stormi slammed her fist on the counter. "He would never have put people in that rocket ship if he believed those boosters were subpar. But what Zero Gravity showed the world was faulty mechanics. They proved that his energy saving boosters were not what he advertised. That his design wasn't ready."

"Your father stated that those weren't his designs," Lincoln said. "Someone had to have hacked the system and we both know it must have been Samantha."

"But why? What does she have to gain from doing that?"

Lincoln lowered his chin. "For starters, if she and Kurt believed you were alive, it was one way to get you to play, and you did do exactly that." He waggled his finger. "I also think that Jeannie wants to take credit for your father's lifework. Her dad has never allowed her to be part of the business. Not where she's wanted to be anyway."

"You mentioned pictures of all of them together. Do we know who initiated contact?"

"It appears David did." Lincoln narrowed his stare. "Well, shit."

"What?"

"I might be grasping at straws, but Samantha's mother would never tell her who her father was and it always bothered her. For years, she tried to find out but always came up empty-handed. She would get mad at me because I wouldn't help her."

"Why wouldn't you?" Stormi jerked her head back. "I'd want to know."

"Because she wanted me to take the risk of illegally hacking into places. I couldn't do that. Not with my military career." Lincoln tapped his finger on the counter. "What if David's her father? What if this started as a threat to expose his paternity, and Jeanie turned it around into using it for her own benefit."

"Are you suggesting that Jeannie is the mastermind behind this? That she's the one who switched the boosters? Caused the explosion?"

"She had access. She had the means. And she'd have the help of Samantha. Especially if that meant she could keep a lid on having a half sister. Or at least control the narrative," Lincoln said. "Samantha's drive for finding her father was only about knowing. Not about some dude staking claim over her. But she's also driven by money and power."

"Jesus. She's going to find fault in your program. Hell, she's going to come in and find me while I'm poking around. She'll plant a tiny piece of evidence that I'll think will be the key in exonerating my dad, but in reality will be the one thing that seals my fate. She'll swoop in, save the day right before Jeannie's innovative rocket boosters are launched into space." Stormi jumped to her feet. "We have to stop these assholes at their own game." She glanced at her watch. "We don't have much time."

He stood, reaching for her, tugging her to his chest. "I'm sorry I lied to you. I won't do it again."

"I can't deal with that right now."

He fanned his thumb across her cheek. "You have to know how much I care about you. It came out of left field, but I don't want this to end."

Her heart betrayed her mind and her emotions. She wanted to stay angry at him forever. "I won't deny that I care about you too." She blinked out a tear. "But right now, all I can focus on is finishing this so I can be reunited with my dad. It's that relationship I need to mend. This one will have to take a back seat."

"I understand." He brushed his lips over her mouth. "I'll wait. I can be a patient man when I want something, and I want you." He patted her bottom. "Now, let's get to work. I picked up more equipment on my way home. I'll put on a pot of coffee while you start setting up."

"You trust me to do that?"

"Babe, I trust you with my life. And my heart," he whispered.

She wished she felt the same.

LINCOLN CRACKED his knuckles and stared at the screens as his program loaded into Zero Gravity's system, overriding the previous one. He glanced at his watch.

He and Stormi had worked through the night to finish the coding. Her ability to copy his language had been more than impressive. It had been downright scary. He wouldn't have been able to complete the project had it not been for her. However, Samantha would be able to see some of the slight variances to how she did things. But that was fine. It was all a trap anyway.

"It will take two hours before this is complete." He leaned back. "How goes things with the hack into Jeannie's computer?"

"Interesting."

"What does that mean?" He rolled his chair closer to Stormi and glanced over her shoulder, scanning the code flashing across her screen.

"I've pulled off three encrypted files so far and dumped them to an external drive. I wanted to finish the scan before I tried opening them, but in the meantime, I've been able to read some of her emails. I've also made copies of all of that."

"And?"

"Well, she's been communicating with Samantha since before your ex met with her father. As a matter of fact." Stormi tapped the keyboard. "According to that correspondence, it was Jeannie who told Samantha that she had what she was looking for and that if Samantha helped her, she'd help Samantha."

"Interesting, but that was eight years ago."

"My father began his work on the rocket boosters about ten years ago."

"Your dad said that Jeannie did spend time in his lab," Lincoln said. "He mentioned that she was always trying to worm her way in, even though her dad tried to keep her out. For a few years, your father felt sorry for her and gave her different things to do. But then David laid into him and threatened to fire him if he kept using Jeannie."

"But you said David had a change of heart and told my dad to let her on the team."

Lincoln nodded. "However, that wasn't with the development of the project. More like a liaison between David, PR, and all the other teams that went into making that rocket take flight. The key here is that Samantha and Jeannie are working together. The question becomes, is David aware of what they are doing and is in on it, or is he oblivious?"

"I'm sure he's just trying to save his own ass. Protect his investment. Zero Gravity has been one step behind other companies. David wants to be the leader."

"That explosion set him back. It had to have pissed him off that his daughter and Samantha, who could also be his kid, fucked him over."

"Kids do some pretty dumb things to get their parents' attention."

"I wouldn't know about that." Lincoln rubbed the back of his neck. "What kinds of things did you do?"

"I married Kurt." She laughed. "But that backfired on me. All it did was bring a bigger divide. My father knew he was a snake. He told me I could come home, but I wasn't to bring that dick with me. I dug my heels into the ground and told my old man to fuck off, something I've regretted for years." She swiped at her cheeks. "When Kara told me my only choice was to fake my death, it killed me in a different way because I knew I'd never be able to see my dad again."

He cupped her chin. "You will be reunited with your father if it's the last thing I do."

His computer sent off a warning bell. "Fuck," he muttered.

"What's wrong?"

He rolled back to his screens. "Someone stopped the implementation of the program." He tapped at the keyboard. "And kicked me out of the upload portal." He tried again, but he was totally frozen out. "Well, they're onto us." He leaned back. "I can't get back in; meanwhile, they've stolen my system through the portal."

"Did the Trojan horse make it inside their system?"

"I have no idea. But even if it did, it doesn't do us much good if I can't get inside." He rolled his neck as he tried the back door. "Well, fuck." He pointed to the screen. "They're uploading a new system now."

"Nothing's unhackable. You know that." She pushed his chair to the side.

He grabbed her wrist. "No. That's what they want us to do. It's a trap."

"How can you be so sure?"

He pointed to the break in the code that appeared on the screen. A break he put there, but it was bigger. More obvious than he'd intentionally made it. "Because that's our invitation. That's part of the Trojan horse. If they loaded it, they will see it. Samantha knows how I operate. Kurt knows you."

"You're going to give up that easily?"

He shook his head. "I'm going to call them out directly."

"I don't follow."

He chuckled as he tapped his cell. "Just listen." The cell rang twice. He tapped the speaker button as he pressed his finger to his lips. "Shhh."

"Lincoln. How are you?" Samantha's voice screeched across the airwaves, making the hair on the back of his neck stand on end.

"Not good," he said. "I have some bad news regarding Zero Gravity."

"I thought you said you'd be done with the coding today?"

"Oh, I am. And I was just about to send it to you through the portal, but I wanted to check on something inside their system first. I wanted to see the hole and how it was created in the first place, making sure it wouldn't happen again."

"I take offense to that since I'm the one who wrote that code to begin with."

Lincoln laughed. "That was a long time ago and

things change. Cybersecurity is different and so is coding. You didn't do anything wrong." He swallowed the bitter taste of that lie. "The problem is someone already uploaded my new system." He learned forward and stared at the code on the screen, studying the break. He had a couple of choices and decided to go the long way in. He moved his cursor down eight lines and found what he was looking for and started typing. He knew Samantha was watching. Or someone she was working with. Maybe Tony. Fucker. But they would be watching the Trojan horse. The break he created for them to delete. Or for him to use to hack in. They wouldn't expect him to go in right under their noses. "I'm looking at it right now. It's my program, only someone fucked with it. There are lines in there that I didn't write and if you were to enter the system, you'd see it too."

"I'm not sure I follow. How could it not be your coding? You're not an easy man to copy. Your style is very unique."

"Thanks for the compliment, but are you near a computer? Can you log in to the system? If you go to the portal and find line 20098, you'll see exactly what I mean."

Stormi scribbled something on a piece of paper.

Is that something Samantha would have written?

Lincoln nodded.

"How the hell did that happen?" Samantha asked. "Who has access to your computer? Or should I be asking, who the fuck have you been sleeping with? You know how sensitive this job is. I can't believe you let that dick of yours cloud your judgment."

Bingo.

Stormi folded her arms and glared between him and the phone on the desk.

"First off, I'm not the one with a cheating problem. That would be you." Lincoln didn't like having this argument with his ex, much less doing it in front of his current girlfriend.

If he could even call Stormi that.

But the whole point was to get Samantha going down that road. To get her to show her hand.

And that's exactly what she was doing.

Now all he had to do was get her to come out of the shadows and show her pretty little face.

He found his way into Zero Gravity's new system and pushed the keyboard over toward Stormi. He scribbled a quick note on a piece of paper.

Find what we need. You have fifteen minutes before they unjumble you.

"Semantics," Samantha said. "This is a fucking mess. It's overwritten the old system completely. It wasn't even backed up."

"There should have been some kind of protection in place in case the system went down. There's got to be a copy of it somewhere. Don't you have it?"

"Not the point, Lincoln. I'm going to have to pull

them offline and go through this myself, line by line. Hell, I might as well write the damn system myself."

"You don't have to do that," Lincoln said. "I can go through it."

"No. You're the whole reason we're in this fucking mess. I have no idea what I'm going to tell the client now. But you're to stay as far away from this as possible. Except I want the name of the person who messed with your code. And don't you fucking lie to me. What she did was criminal."

"I'll deal with her."

"Like hell. She put my company at risk. Left me wide-open for all sorts of legal issues. I'm turning her in, unless you want to take the fall for her, because that's exactly what will happen," Samantha said.

His printer hummed to life.

Stormi leaned back, folded her arms over her chest, and smiled.

"Give me twenty-four hours, and then I'll give up her name."

"You've got two hours; otherwise, I'm giving up yours." The line went dead.

"What did you find?" He turned Stormi's chair, pressing his hands on her armrests.

"The goddamn fucking golden ticket, that's what." She clasped her hands on his cheeks and smacked her lips over his mouth. "I got my father's original files. All of them. Every single last one."

"How can you be so sure?"

"Look for yourself." She jerked her thumb over her shoulder. "She had to do a data dump of the old system. While she was busy looking at your coding and what you did, I quickly opened, printed, and emailed it to me, you, and Kara. I made sure I closed it all out and then dumped it back into the abyss."

Quickly, he snagged a few pages from the printout. "We're going to need confirmation from your father that this is his rocket boosters."

"There were two files. One front and center, tucked away in a digital hallway. But it was the one that was hidden that was clearly marked. I took a chance and peeked inside the one that was filed with letters and numbers that my father would use. That's the one I printed. Not the one I believe she was trying to bait us with."

"I hope you're right." He opened his top drawer and snagged his weapon, waving it over one of his screens. "Because we have unwanted company and the bitch brought Tony." He leaned over and tapped a few keystrokes. "At the back door we have David and his daughter, so we're outnumbered." He lifted his cell and sent a message to Tal and a second one to Jimmy. "I don't know about David or Jeannie and what kind of training they have with weapons. But Tony spent four years in the British Navy. And Samantha is damn good with a gun. I know that because I taught her how to shoot." He took Stormi by the shoulders. "Can you handle a weapon?"

"Nope."

He took a second gun from his collection and placed it in her hands. "It's pretty simple. Aim and pull the trigger. Just don't shoot me, okay?"

"I hate guns."

"Don't care. If push comes to shove and it's a matter of your life or theirs, use it. Otherwise, pretend it's not shoved in your pants." He yanked the back of her jeans and placed it in the small of her back before pulling her shirt over it. "Let me do the talking."

"You should know that when I'm nervous, I tend to shoot my mouth off."

"Wonderful," he said under his breath. He snagged the printout.

"What are you doing?" She glared.

"I will give it to them if they ask for it. The bigger problem will be the emails. Not sure how they will handle that because if they know you printed it, they will know you emailed it."

"Um, Lincoln. They didn't come here to collect anything." She pointed to the screens. "They came here to kill us. By fire."

He glanced up. His heart pulsated as he watched the front of his house flicker with flames. They crawled up the side of his home like a snake. He tapped a few keystrokes. The back of the house was already engulfed.

Crash.

Smash.

The sound of glass breaking echoed in the background.

More shattering glass filled his ears. The roar of a raging fire filled his ears.

The window to the office crackled as a bottle with a rag soaked with gas was hurled into the room.

"Look out!" He shoved her to the side.

The curtains caught fire.

"Can you still access my system?"

"Yeah. But we have to get out of here." He tugged at her arm.

"No. You need to open lines of communication between our two systems. You need to data dump this into mine. I don't think mine will be able to handle all of it, so just route the important stuff." She pressed her hand on the door. "Jesus, it's burning hot already. Do the dump now, and then we'll crawl out the window."

As quickly as he could, he hooked into her system. All he needed was his security files and the information on Zero Gravity. He sent those and then made a beeline for the window just as another firebomb came hurling at him. He ducked, tackling her to the floor.

She screamed. "What the hell was that?"

"Our death sentence," he managed as he rolled left and right, dousing the fire that had managed to stick to their clothing. "Stay as low as you can." He crawled toward the window, keeping her close. He lifted his head. Flames and smoke were everywhere.

The sound of the door slamming against the wall

caught his attention. He glanced over his shoulder. Someone wearing fire gear and an oxygen mask entered the room.

Thank God.

Only that thought lasted ten seconds.

Whoever that person was raised a large object and before Lincoln could blink, the world went black.

CHAPTER FOURTEEN

Stormi groaned and blinked open her eyes. Her head bobbled as she tried to focus on her surroundings. She had absolutely no idea where she was. The last thing she remembered was being surrounded by flames. Panic seized her heart. Her breath came in short, choppy pants.

"Try to relax, babe. Take long, deep breaths. In through your nose, out through your mouth," Lincoln said.

She lifted her head. "Lincoln," she whispered. His face was covered in bruises, blood, and dirt. He sat in a chair directly across from her, with his hands behind his back. "Where are we? Are you okay?"

"I'm no worse for the wear," he said. "I think we're somewhere in the Zero Gravity facilities. I woke up during the transport. It took twelve minutes after that to get here. They blindfolded us. But we went up a flight of stairs, into an elevator, and down. But honestly, I can't be sure. I'm making an educated guess."

"Do you think they were trying to make it look like we died in a house fire?" She swallowed. It tasted like a combination of tar and burnt toast.

"Perhaps, but it would be hard without two bodies and it doesn't make a whole lot of sense."

She shivered. "Have you seen anyone since we've been here?"

"You certainly ask a lot of questions." He arched a brow. "To answer what I think you want to know and that's who our captors are, the only face I've seen is Samantha's."

The sound of a heavy metal door scraping against the floor scratched at her ears like nails against a chalkboard. God, she hated that noise.

"Oh, goodie. You're both awake." Samantha snagged a chair and dragged it across the tile floor. She stopped four feet in front of them, turned the chair, and straddled it.

She was a pretty woman, a little rough around the edges with her dark boots that laced up to her knee. Her jet-black hair and dark makeup reminded Stormi of the scientist on that TV show about the Navy police. It was a very different look than her own, so that comment about Lincoln having a type certainly didn't have anything to do with a woman's appearance.

"What the fuck are you up to, Samantha? Because I

can't figure it out. I used to think you were one of the smartest people I knew. But this just feels about as dumb as a rock."

Samantha chuckled as she shook her head. "It was a combination of panic and scrounging for time. That fire bought us a day. Maybe two."

"For what, exactly?"

"To form a new plan. Create a new fall guy." Samantha waggled her finger in the direction of Stormi. "Thanks to your little girlfriend, the Feds now know that Zero Gravity fucked her father up the ass." Samantha shrugged. "That's really not my problem. I honestly don't give a shit about that, except for the money." She pursed her lips.

"What money?" Stormi asked.

"Ah, she speaks." Samantha stood and inched closer. "I knew Lincoln would be attracted to your brain. I mean, he was already salivating over your coding. He did that three years ago when I showed it to him. It was all *Twister* this and *Twister* that. He was beyond impressed with your capabilities. And I warned Kurt you could be a problem, but Kurt figured you were so frigid and singularly focused that you wouldn't even notice Lincoln." Samantha ran her fingers through Stormi's hair.

"Don't fucking touch her," Lincoln said behind gritted teeth.

"Oh, possessive over her already, I see." Samantha leaned closer. Her hot breath heated Stormi's cheek.

"He falls in love so hard and fast. It's kind of pathetic."

"You hurt her, and I will strangle the life out of you with my bare hands," Lincoln said, his voice more of a growl.

Samantha laughed. "Because you could ever lay a hand on a woman." She continued to run her fingers through Stormi's hair, petting her as if she were a puppy. "Lincoln might be full of muscles and be a badass, but he couldn't raise a finger to a female. Goes against some gentleman honor code he has."

"Well, you're no fucking woman, so I'd have no problem with it at all," he mumbled. "What the hell do you want, Samantha?"

Samantha yanked a weapon from an ankle holster. She ran it up the side of Stormi's arm, neck, and face.

The cold metal seeped through Stormi's skin and into her bloodstream.

"When I was a little girl, I wanted a father who loved me. But my mom couldn't give me that. She wouldn't tell me who he was. Not even a hint. So, when I learned he knew of me all along, but couldn't be bothered, I wanted a piece of his action."

"What does this have to do with your plans for us?" Stormi twisted her wrists. She winced as the plastic ties cut into her skin.

"Shut up, bitch." The back of Samantha's hand came across Stormi's cheek with a *crack* and a *thud*. The taste of metal filled Stormi's mouth.

"You're going to pay for that." Lincoln shifted in his chair, moving it a few inches closer.

"Do you want to know what I've got in store for you or not? Because I can just get on with it, or I can tell you." Samantha pressed her gun against Stormi's temple.

"All right. We'll be quiet." Lincoln nodded.

"Good." Samantha held Stormi's head, with the cold metal still pressed against her skin.

Stormi couldn't take in a deep breath. Hell, she could barely suck in any oxygen at all. Panic was close to setting in. She focused on Lincoln, holding his gaze. His soft blue eyes were about the only thing keeping her from losing her damn mind.

"When I learned David Caulkin was my father and that I had a half sister, well, I wasn't going to let that go," Samantha said. "The first couple of meetings didn't go well. David didn't want to have anything to do with me." She shrugged. "Neither did Jeannie. In some ways, they still don't. But I showed them my value over the years, especially with that first security system."

"You mean the one Stormi hacked into, stole documents, and leaked them," Lincoln said, cocking his head.

"That was unfortunate, but it was the hole that allowed me to see inside and give Jeannie what she needed so she could make sure that launch failed, steal the rocker booster plans, and make them her own." Samantha smiled triumphantly.

"David didn't know you did that?" Stormi asked.

"Not at first. But he does now and he's on board. He'd rather his kid get all the glory than some old fool who's dead now anyway." Samantha tugged at Stormi's hair. "But you had to go steal those plans with his name on them and send them to your friend at the FBI. One of the reasons you couldn't die in that fire. I mean, you're already dead. We thought about leaving Lincoln there, but the fire trucks were a little too close. We figured it was possible they could save him."

"So, what now? Make us disappear?" Stormi asked.

"Wow. She's not as smart as I thought she'd be." Samantha released her grip and strolled a few paces closer to Lincoln. "Actually, Lincoln here will put a bullet in you because you betrayed him. Got to love AI. We'll get the whole thing on video for the world to see."

"Oh really. Interesting. Now, how did she betray me?" Lincoln asked.

"Those documents will turn out to be forged. She lied to you and we all know how much you loathe a liar." Samantha tossed her head back and laughed. "David and Jeannie are upstairs right now creating a new set of documents. Ones that will be slightly different, but ones that will be placed on our server and which we will be able to prove without a doubt are the originals. And without her father or anyone else on his team to state otherwise, she doesn't have a leg to stand on. Not to mention, new evidence will be found regarding Kurt's case. He'll be exonerated, and in death, she'll be nothing but a criminal who almost got away with it."

"Damn, that's quite a good piece of fiction. Too bad it's all bullshit and we still have an ace up our sleeves." Lincoln grinned from ear to ear. "You have always seriously underestimated me, which is fine. But now you've gone and underestimated my girlfriend. That just pisses me off. Especially when she's better than you." He leaned forward. "At everything."

Samantha stomped across the room. She shoved her weapon into his gut.

He groaned.

"You don't want to fuck with me, Lincoln."

"But I already have," he said. "Are you running the new security program? The one I wrote?"

"Tony ran a diagnostic. There is nothing in that program that can hurt me." She leaned closer. "Besides, he's finishing up his and that will be loaded soon enough. It's all good."

Stormi caught Lincoln's gaze. The Trojan horse embedded in the security system was meant as a distraction for Samantha. She was supposed to see it and spend time deleting it, giving Lincoln and Stormi a chance to search the digital halls. But that's not what happened.

Now that the program was running at full speed, the Trojan horse had not only been activated but was seeping into the system like the Black Plague. When Lincoln first proposed the idea, they both thought all they had to do was make it look real, but Lincoln believed Samantha—if and when she saw the Trojan horse—would see right through an empty threat. So, he made it real.

And now it was slowly opening Zero Gravity to one outside threat after the other.

Lincoln had the audacity to wink the moment Samantha's back was turned.

"I just want to make sure I have this straight," Lincoln said. "You're going to kill Stormi, making it look like I did it. You're going to set her up to take the fall for things Kurt did, as if she'd been the mastermind all along, not him. But you haven't explained what you're going to do with me?"

Samantha tapped the weapon to her temple. "You know, we're still exploring our options. You're not the type of man to blow your own brains out, so I'm not sure that's the right plan. We're thinking perhaps a shoot-out and you get caught in the crossfire."

"And how will you make that happen?"

"Oh, I'm thinking we'll call the police. Report a break-in. Perhaps you fire at them and leave them no other choice but to fire back." Samantha laughed. "Yeah. That's the ticket."

Stormi twisted her wrists again, but the plastic restraints were too tight. "You won't get away with this. Your plan is utterly absurd."

"Sometimes you need the ridiculous to make sense of those things that make no sense at all." Samantha shrugged. "I best go check on how things are going upstairs and also with the investigation into the fire at Lincoln's place. I suspect we only have a few more hours before we have to set this plan in motion." Samantha turned and strolled toward the door like she didn't have a care in the world.

Stormi opened her mouth, but Lincoln shook his head and mouthed, *Don't say a word. They're listening.*

She swallowed the bitter taste of being doomed.

LINCOLN TRUSTED THREE THINGS. First and foremost, his instincts.

Second, his team.

Today, that meant Tal, his buddies at search and rescue, and Jimmy.

And finally, his abilities both in the field and behind a computer screen.

He twisted his arms. His wrists were raw and bleeding from trying to break free from his restraints. He glanced around the room. There was one exit. Above the door was a security camera. It was too high for him to take out from his chair. In the far-right corner was a small desk with a laptop.

In the center of the room were him and Stormi.

There was nothing else.

That was good and bad because he could not communicate with the outside world unless he got to that computer. But if he did that without taking out the security camera, he'd be fucked.

"You sure know how to pick them," Stormi muttered.

"I'm not sure what you mean by that." He let out a long breath. It had been approximately fifteen minutes since Samantha left the room. He suspected she was watching. The silence had probably frustrated the hell out of her, but so would this topic of conversation, so he might as well run with it.

"Women." Stormi arched a brow. "Your ex is interesting. Not what I expected at all."

He laughed. "Why? Outside of the fact she's a total bitch and I didn't see it for five fucking years."

Stormi's gaze dropped to his toes and then eased back up his body like a laser on a mission. "Look at you. You're the poster child for the clean-cut boy next door with your short blond hair, sweet blue eyes, and basic clothes. I get you're a badass military man, but you don't look the part. You look like a fucking Boy Scout and she looks like a misunderstood, angry girl with daddy issues."

"I didn't always look like this." He cocked his head. "When I first met Tal, I wore black eyeliner, had hair down to my shoulders, and dressed like a bum. Of course, I was living on the streets and a criminal, so there was that."

The video light on the laptop lit up.

He narrowed his eyes and focused on the screen.

There was no reason for that to happen. Not unless the security camera wasn't working.

But then why would the laptop suddenly light up?

A pop-up menu appeared with a message.

Backup has arrived. Hang tight. Don't do anything stupid.

Just as quickly as the message illuminated the screen, it disappeared. So did the video light.

Jimmy.

It had to have been Jimmy. He was the only one who had the capabilities to hack into the system, find the Trojan horse, and use it to weave in and out of Zero Gravity until he found Lincoln and Stormi.

Of course, he couldn't have done it without Tal because Lincoln was sure Jimmy would have reached out after that last text. Or vice versa.

The cavalry was on the way.

They had to be.

But he couldn't say a fucking word to Stormi. Shit. She was going to be pissed. Again.

He was fucking tired of having the woman he cared about being angry at him because he kept secrets.

"I'd love to see a picture of that," Stormi said.

"When we get out of here, I'll dig one up for you. But you have to promise not to laugh."

"I will make no such promise." A few tears dribbled down her cheeks.

God, he wished he could tell her it was going to be okay. But even knowing someone was on the way to rescue them, he couldn't promise her anything. For all he knew, that message was a trick, something he had to consider.

Behind him, the door flung open.

He jerked his head as Jimmy raced down the ten steps.

"I've got the security camera going on a five-minute loop in this room. But we've got to hurry." Jimmy quickly cut through Stormi's ties.

"Who are you?" Stormi asked as she rubbed her wrists.

"Special Agent James Hallenbeck, at your service, ma'am," Jimmy said. "I've been working with your father. Now, let's move." He cut through Lincoln's plastic restraints. "Tal, Brayden, Blaze, Brock, and Zeke are all covering the perimeter."

"Why aren't we taking them out?" Stormi asked.

"A girl who wants vengeance." Jimmy chuckled as he took her by the arm and raced up the steps. "That Trojan horse program is finding me a whole lot more than just Jeannie stealing your father's rocket booster design and then switching it out with a faulty one, causing that explosion. But right now, all that matters is getting you to safety."

"What's the plan?" Lincoln took Stormi's hand and ran down the hallway, following Jimmy.

"Everything will fall apart for them without you two and without the forged documentation. Once the Trojan horse has finished loading everything into my system, me and my team, along with the local police, will arrest David, Jeannie, Tony, and Samantha. The four of them will go away for a very long…" Jimmy skidded to a stop. "Motherfucker."

Lincoln pushed Stormi behind him. "Samantha, put that thing down. You don't want to do this. It's over."

Bang!

* * *

STORMI SCREAMED.

Jimmy dropped to his knees, clutching his gut. Blood trickled between his fingers.

Stormi's gaze shifted between Samantha and Jimmy.

"You didn't have to do that." Lincoln took Jimmy by the shoulders and eased him down to the floor. "Stormi, put as much pressure as possible on his wound."

"Aw, look at you." Samantha laughed. "Aren't you cute, trying to save a dead man."

"He's got a wife. Kids. Let him go. It's me you want anyway," Lincoln said.

"And your bitch girlfriend." Samantha cocked her head.

"I'd be careful who you call bitch," Stormi muttered as she pressed her hands on Jimmy's stomach.

Jimmy shifted to the side, showing off a second weapon.

Stormi swallowed. She slinked her fingers around the butt of the gun.

"You don't want to piss me off any more than I already am. Trust me, I'll shoot you and not bat an eyelash," Samantha said.

"So will I." With an unsteady hand, Stormi raised the weapon, pointed it at Samantha's chest, and pulled the trigger.

Bang!

Samantha's eyes grew wide. Her gun slipped from her fingertips. She glanced down at her chest, then back to Stormi. "I can't believe you fucking shot me." Blood trickled out of Samantha's mouth as she gurgled and coughed, stumbling backward. "Unbelievable." She fell to the floor, taking her last breath.

"Jimmy. Stay with us, man." Lincoln tore off his shirt and pushed it over his bloody abdomen. "Do you have a cell?"

Jimmy nodded. "But your buddies are right behind you," he said weakly.

"Already called it in. The ambulance should be here in less than five. Weston's outside waiting to show them the way." Tal rested his hand on Lincoln's shoulder. "Damn. She's a good shot." Tal pushed him aside and took over attending to Jimmy's wounds.

Stormi covered her face. A guttural sob filled her throat.

"Hey there." Lincoln's strong arms wrapped around

her body, lifting her onto his lap. He kissed her temple. "It's okay. Let it all out."

"I killed her," she whispered. "I took a life. How will I ever live with myself?"

"Oh, sweetheart." Lincoln held her tighter. "I wish I could say you won't have nightmares. Or that this won't affect you, because it will. But don't forget, she tried to kill Jimmy, and she would have killed both of us if you hadn't pulled that trigger."

"I know. I know, but that doesn't take away the pain in my chest. I didn't even think. I just did it."

"Because you acted on instinct." He cupped her face. "I'm not proud of the fact that I've taken human life. It always haunts me."

A gentle touch squeezed her leg. "I know that this will be a struggle," Jimmy said weakly. "Whether I make it or not, my family will be grateful to you."

"You've got to make it." Stormi swiped at her face. "You have to fight."

"Trust me. I am." Jimmy smiled.

The sound of boots hitting the tile floor filled the air. She glanced over Lincoln's shoulder. The paramedics raced in their direction.

"Is this over? Can I see my father?" she asked no one in particular.

"Unfortunately, the FBI works slowly." Weston, a local police officer, appeared behind the paramedics. "It might take a day or two. There will be questioning and lots of red tape to jump through. And there is the question of your identity and how to handle that."

More tears flowed. She couldn't stop them if she tried.

"Babe, I'll be with you every step of the way," Lincoln whispered as he helped her to a standing position.

The paramedics lifted Jimmy onto the gurney. He reached for her hand. "And remember this. You set the record straight when it came to your father. And this company. You did a good thing. Don't forget that."

"We've got to roll," the paramedic said.

She leaned into Lincoln's strong frame. "I kind of want to go back to being a librarian."

Lincoln chuckled. "Come on. Unfortunately, it's going to be a long few days of interviews."

She glanced up, catching his soulful, loving gaze. "Thank you."

"For what?"

"Searching for the truth. Searching for the real me, even though I didn't make it easy."

He kissed her temple. "Babe, from the moment I met you, I was hooked and now you're never getting rid me."

"I wouldn't want to." She patted his chest. "But if I ever catch you stealing my eyeliner, we're going to have a problem."

CHAPTER FIFTEEN

Stormi blew out a puff of air as she fiddled with the paper coffee mug. "I'm sorry about what happened."

"It's not your fault," Norman said, reaching across the table and taking her hand.

The stale smell of antiseptic filled her nostrils. She hated hospitals and this was the last place she'd wanted to have this conversation. She wasn't entirely sure how Norman and Brad had learned she was here, but she suspected Lincoln might have had something to do with it.

She couldn't be mad at him for that. Norman and his son had the right to closure, and she had the power to give it to them.

"My wife and her father brought this on themselves." Norman glanced toward his son. "Is there anything you want to say or ask?"

“This might seem like a weird question. But it’s similar to what I asked Mr. Ross,” Brad said.

“What did you ask him?” Stormi tilted her head.

“If I would still be allowed to date his daughter after everything that happened.” Brad slumped his shoulders.

“You’re not guilty of anything,” Lincoln said. “Children are not the sum of their parents’ sins and I know what Tal and Heather told you. You’re welcome in their home.”

“My son’s also worried about what this might do to his chances of getting into the Air Force Academy,” Norman said.

“It’s not going to affect you negatively at all.” Lincoln squeezed Brad’s biceps. “The man we came to see today, he’s with the FBI. I also know a few people with the CIA, DEA, and other government agencies. As well as people high up in the military. If your grades are good enough, and you have what they want, you’ll get in.” Lincoln leaned forward. “I also have a couple of friends who used to be fire protection specialists. And your dad says that’s what you’re considering. If you’d like, I can set up a meeting.”

“I’d like that very much.” Brad nodded. “Thank you. But I still haven’t had the chance to ask Stormi my question.”

“What is it?” Stormi asked.

“Am I welcome in the library? To volunteer for the

rest of the summer? I need twenty more hours," Brad said.

"Of course." Stormi smiled.

"Thanks for taking the time to meet with us." Norman stood. "Now all I have to do is find a job."

"Perhaps we should talk." Lincoln stretched out his hand. "I'm going to be starting my company. Stormi will be part of it, but she'll be keeping her job at the library, and I'll be needing some marketing help. I can't pay what Zero Gravity was, but it would be a start."

"I like the sound of that," Norman said. "I'll be in touch."

Stormi leaned into Lincoln's strong body and watched father and son step through the electric doors and out of the hospital. She sucked in a deep breath. "Guess I better go see Jimmy."

"Do you want me to go with you?" Lincoln asked.

She shook her head. "No. I need to do this on my own." It had been three days since she'd been held captive by Samantha. Three days since she'd shot and killed a human being. Three days since Jimmy had nearly died.

And she still hadn't been able to see her father.

According to the new FBI agent in charge of her dad's case, that might not happen for a few more days while they shuffle through all the shit that had come out of Zero Gravity.

The company had been shut down for good.

David ended up cooperating with the FBI, hoping

to receive a lesser sentence. Turns out, his daughters were blackmailing him. But that didn't make him less culpable. Not when it came to the explosion and deaths of Dante's team.

Jeannie, on the other hand, was doing her best to place all the blame on Samantha, a dead woman.

But with David giving up all the information, Jeannie was going to be facing life in prison.

Tony, Samantha's sidekick, was sent back to the UK and faced all sorts of charges there. He won't be getting out of prison anytime soon.

And Kurt would continue to rot in his own little hell, knowing his wife, now soon-to-be ex-wife, had turned on him and was alive and well, living the dream.

Lincoln palmed her cheek. "I'll be right out here if you need me."

The last three days were filled with interview after interview. There were questions from the local police, the FBI, the CIA, and even NASA. While she never felt as though she was the criminal, they all wanted to know her role, how she got her information, why she did what she did, and how she knew what she knew. It was all a delicate dance.

If it had not been for Lincoln, she would have surely lost her mind. He'd become her rock. He held her at night and not once judged when the nightmares came.

And they came every night, making her kick, scream, and cry.

He told her they were normal. That he'd suffered them too. And that soon enough, they would go away.

God, she hoped.

But her nightmares weren't solely connected to the fact she'd taken a woman's life. No. Deep down she understood what she'd done and that if she hadn't, she, Lincoln, and Jimmy probably wouldn't be breathing.

She placed her hand on her stomach and inhaled. Nor would her little one and that was the crux of her bad dreams.

"Thank you." She raised up on tiptoe and kissed his cheek. She owed him so much. More importantly, she owed him one more heavy dose of the truth. "When I'm done here, can we go for a walk? I need to talk to you."

"Of course." He smiled.

She turned and headed down the hallway until she found Jimmy's room. She sucked in a deep breath and pulled back the curtain.

"Stormi. I'm so glad you came." Jimmy adjusted himself on the hospital bed. Sitting by his side was a beautiful young woman. "This is my wife, Hillary."

"It's so nice to finally meet you." Hillary jumped off the bed and squeezed Stormi tight.

"I'm so sorry about what happened," Stormi managed.

"You've got nothing to apologize for." Hillary waved her hand. "I'm just glad all the good guys are okay." Hillary smiled. "Where's Lincoln? I wanted to meet him. My sister says he's quite the sexy Brit."

"You just want to hear his accent." Jimmy laughed.

"Oh, his accent is yummy." Stormi rested her hip against the chair. "He's in the waiting room. We have something we need to take care of, and then I'll send him in."

"That sound ominous and interesting all at the same time," Hillary said.

"Not really. It's just been a long few days and it could be a few more days before I get to be reunited with my dad." Stormi reached for her hair and twisted it between her fingers.

"They haven't let me speak to your dad since this happened," Jimmy said. "I'm sure he's just as frustrated as you are. But you'll never be separated again."

"Listen. They're going to let Jimmy out of this place tomorrow. Would you and Lincoln like to come over for dinner next week? I'll have my sister Madison and her husband Brayden over."

"I'm sure Lincoln would love that. I know he and Brayden have a history." Stormi smiled, taking Jimmy's hand. "I can't thank you enough for everything you did for me." Tears burned the corners of her eyes. "I'm just sorry it resulted in your getting shot."

"Unfortunately, that goes with the territory." He squeezed her hand. "A little piece of advice," he said. "Don't hold on to the demons like a badge of honor. I've done what you have, but I'm trained to do it. Even though the consequences still stick with a person, I have a different mindset because of my career. What you need to do is remember the difference between good people who make a choice to survive and bad people who choose to be evil." He arched a brow. "The distinction is important."

"I'm getting there." She nodded. "Heather recommended a good therapist and Lincoln's been incredibly supportive." But Stormi had to wonder if it all boiled down to being honest. Her nightmare was always the same. She held the gun in her fingertips. She was about to pull the trigger when Samantha held up her baby, preventing her from doing what was necessary.

Samantha won.

And right in front of Stormi's eyes, Samantha killed her precious child.

"He's a good man and I suspect he loves you very much," Jimmy said.

She swallowed her emotions. Love was a strong word. It didn't matter that her heart felt it so strongly it pulsated through her system like rain falling from the sky. "It's too soon for that kind of talk."

"It's never too soon when it's right." Hillary palmed her cheek. "Go. Spend time with your man. We'll see you next week."

Now all she had to do was tell Lincoln they were going to be bonded together in such a way that might make him run for the hills.

* * *

LINCOLN PULLED out his cell and tapped Dante's contact information.

"Hey, son," Dante said.

Lincoln's heart swelled. It was a silly sensation. Especially when it was simply an expression of speech. Dante didn't mean anything by it.

"Where are you?" Lincoln asked.

"About forty minutes away."

"Okay. She's in with Jimmy now. Then she wants to go for a walk and chat about something. I'll take her to the courtyard in the center of the hospital. There's a nice garden. You can meet us there."

"Sounds like a good plan," Dante said. "How's she doing?"

"She has good and bad moments." Lincoln ran a hand over his mouth. It killed him every time she had a nightmare, and she had them every night. Sometimes two and three times a night. Taking a life, even when it was in self-defense, wasn't something a person could turn around and live with. Most people who owned guns thought if they had to pull the trigger in defense of themselves or their family, it would be a no-brainer.

But they never took into account the aftermath.

"I think seeing Jimmy and then being with you will help her," Lincoln said. "Right now, she can't put all the good that came out of her actions in her mind."

"Are you kidding? She's alive. You're alive. How is that not good?"

Lincoln chuckled. "It's awesome. But she's holding

on to it, and the only thing I can think of is because she hasn't seen you. She'll get there. She just needs time."

"I'm sure you're right," Dante said. "I'll see you soon." The line went dead.

Lincoln stuffed his cell in his back pocket. He knew two things.

First, he loved Stormi with every fiber of his being.

And he'd crumble without her in his life.

The sound of her heels clicking on the tile tickled his ears. He smiled. "Hey, you." He stretched out his arms. "How did it go?"

"Really well." She fell into his embrace, resting her head on his shoulder. "Jimmy looks well, and I got to meet his wife."

"I know her sister, Madison. Sweet girl." Lincoln took her hand and led her through the hospital corridor toward the courtyard. "Both she and Brayden have been through a lot." He pushed open the door. The bright sun beat down on his face. "Why don't we sit over there."

She sat across from him on the picnic table, fiddling with her thumbnail, glancing between her hands, the sky, and the tree to her right.

"What's going on?" Lincoln asked, reaching across the table, taking her hands. He lifted them and pressed his lips against her warm skin. "I know these last few days have been a struggle. I don't want to make it harder, but I'm starting to worry that something else is troubling you."

"Something is." She nodded. "I haven't been completely honest with you about something."

"Okay. What?"

"It goes back to when we first met," she said.

"I'm listening." He ran his thumb over her palm.

"I should have told you the first time we slept together. It was wrong of me." A tear rolled down her pretty face.

He reached out and wiped it away. "Whatever it is, I'm sure it isn't a big deal. Or doesn't even matter anymore." He lifted her chin. "I care so much about you. More than I ever expected. Actually, not to scare you away, but I love you, Stormi. With all that I am."

"You what?" She blinked wildly. "You did not just say you love me?"

He eased to the other side of the table and stared into her questioning eyes. "But I did."

Her lips parted and she gasped.

He chuckled.

"It's not funny," she whispered.

"No. It's not. But I often react that way when I'm feeling a little vulnerable and I have no idea how you feel." He arched a brow. His heart dropped like a brick to his toes. "Do you love me back?"

"I do love you," she said. "But that doesn't change the fact I neglected to tell you something very important."

"Hello, my child," Stormi's father appeared with outstretched arms.

She glanced over her shoulder. "Daddy, you're going to have to wait a minute."

Dante scowled.

"Did you seriously just put your father off? I worked very hard to make this surprise—"

"I'm pregnant." She took Lincoln's hand and placed it over her stomach. "I should have told you I wasn't taking birth control. Every time we had sex, I kept meaning to tell you. It got to the point that I was like, well, I've already done the dance, what difference does it make now, and it won't happen anyway."

His mouth dropped open. He glanced between his hand on her belly, her father, and back to her beautiful eyes.

"I didn't get pregnant on purpose. It certainly wasn't to trap you. I never expected to fall in love with you. And I'm literally shocked to hear you say those words—"

"Anyone ever tell you that you talk too much?" He leaned in and pressed his lips gently over her mouth. "I love you. I don't care how we got to this point. I'm happy about the baby. I want it. And I want you. The only thing that needs to change in our lives is that damn bed of yours. It sucks."

"And the fact that I'm going to leave your embrace so I can go hug my daddy. I haven't done that in years." She kissed him. Hard. And with intent. Only, it didn't last nearly long enough. She leaped from the bench and raced the ten paces to her father's outstretched arms. "Daddy!"

"I'm going to be a grandfather?" He hugged her tightly. "Is there going to be a wedding? Do I get to walk you down the aisle this time?"

"Guess I better go buy a ring." Lincoln laughed.

"I need to get officially divorced." She cupped her father's face. "I can't believe you're really here. How long can you stay?"

Lincoln strolled closer to his family.

Family.

"I told your dad he could stay with us until he found a place to live."

She jerked her head back. "You're moving here?"

"I considered it. But now that you two are getting married and having a baby, it's a done deal." Dante smiled.

Stormi wrapped one arm around Lincoln and the other around Dante.

Lincoln kissed her temple. "I promise to love you forever." When he'd moved to the States, he'd been a broken man. He'd been searching for the pieces that would make him whole. What he found was more than the perfect woman. He found his soulmate.

Stormi was the key that unlocked his heart and showed him what true happiness was all about.

EPILOGUE

ONE YEAR LATER...

"Mommy's home." Stormi tossed her keys on the table next to the front door and raced through the house in search of her baby. "Where's my little bundle of joy?"

"Oh, is that all you care about?" Lincoln stood in the middle of the kitchen, holding their child over his shoulder as he patted the baby's back, bouncing up and down. "No hugs and kisses for Daddy?"

"I'll get to you in a minute. Right now, I want that cheeky kid of ours." She dumped her purse on the counter and lifted little Talon Dante off his father's shoulder and smacked her lips against his chubby little cheeks. "Were you a good boy for Daddy and Grandpa?" She closed her eyes and inhaled the sweet smell of baby. It was the most intoxicating scent she'd ever experienced. It was one part snow, one part sunshine, and one part rain.

"Tal is always a good boy for his dad." Lincoln leaned over and pressed his lips on her mouth.

Tal giggled and kicked his legs wildly.

"Sorry I was late." She set Tal in the jumper seat on the floor, handing him his favorite rattle. She stared at his face. He was the spitting image of his father. Blue eyes. Blond hair. And all the sweetness. "I had to stop by the drugstore on the way home." She glanced around. "Where's my dad?"

"He had a date." Lincoln cocked his head. "Left about ten minutes ago." He waved his hand toward the oven. "But he did make his famous casserole thing. Why won't he tell me what the hell is in it?"

She laughed. "It's nothing special. Chicken. Rice. Cream of chicken soup. A few different kinds of cheeses. Some spices."

"Well, it's freaking delicious." Lincoln rubbed his belly. "And I'm starting to get fat."

"I just lost all my baby fat and now I fear in six months I won't be able to see my feet again." She dug into her purse and pulled out the home pregnancy test. "Even with birth control, you have super sperm."

"Excuse me?" He held the little box in his hands and blinked. "Are you sure?"

"No. But I'm two weeks late."

"You got your period once since you had that one. How can you be late already?"

"Do you really need a lesson in the birds and the bees?" She grabbed the box. "For a forty-one-year-old man, who has a genius IQ, you can be kind of stupid sometimes." She marched down the hallway.

"Where are you going?"

"To find out if we're having baby number two or not."

"You know, I'd be okay with that. I mean, I am getting to be an old man," he yelled.

"I know. I can see the gray hair." She slammed the bathroom door. She wasn't upset by the prospect of being pregnant again. Not at all. She wanted another child. But she hadn't expected it to happen so fast. She'd just gone back to the library, a job she truly loved.

Their cybersecurity company was finally turning a profit, something they desperately needed. And everything with Zero Gravity was behind them. Another kid would be a blessing. She'd just wanted five minutes to breathe.

Knock. Knock.

"I'm almost done."

"For the record, I don't have gray hair."

She laughed, setting the test on the sink. It would take a few minutes. She pulled open the door. Palming her husband's cheek, she smiled. "Yeah, you do."

"Are you not happy about the idea of having another one?"

"No. I'd be thrilled with it. But it would have been nice to have another month or two to relax. We just finally put everything else behind us. Things are running smoothly. I wanted to bask in that glory a little while longer."

"One thing we never talked about is how many kids do we want?"

She arched a brow. "I never thought I'd say this, but I love babies. And we make spectacular-looking ones. At least little Tal is adorable."

"That doesn't answer my question, because if you are pregnant, and if you want it to be the last one, I can make sure that happens."

"Not many men would offer to do that."

He winced. "Can't say it's high on my agenda. But you're the one who has to carry and birth the children. It's the least I can do."

"Well, I don't know if two will be enough for me." Her heart flew right out of her mouth. "I kind of can't believe I said that."

"Me neither." He brushed his lips over her mouth. "I love you. But if we get to four, I'm cutting you off."

"That sounds reasonable." She glanced over her shoulder. "Shall we find out if Tal is going to be a big brother?"

"Let's do it."

She swallowed as she lifted the stick. She smiled. "Guess I won't be having wine with dinner."

Thank you for reading *Searching for Stormi.* Please feel

free to leave an honest review. For more information, please check out my other books!

Grab a glass of vino, kick back, relax, and let the romance roll in…

Sign up for my Newsletter (https://dl.bookfunnel.com/82gm8b9k4y) where I often give away free books before publication.

Join my private Facebook group (https://www.facebook.com/groups/191706547909047/) where I post exclusive excerpts and discuss all things murder and love!

ALSO BY JEN TALTY

Fallport Rescue Operations

Searching for Madison

Searching for Haven

Searching for Pandora

Searching for Stormi

Brand new series: SAFE HARBOR!

Mine To Keep

Mine To Save

Mine To Protect

Mine to Hold

Mine to Love

Check out LOVE IN THE ADIRONDACKS!

Shattered Dreams

An Inconvenient Flame

The Wedding Driver

Clear Blue Sky

Blue Moon

Before the Storm

NY STATE TROOPER SERIES (also set in the Adirondacks!)

In Two Weeks

Dark Water

Deadly Secrets

Murder in Paradise Bay

To Protect His own

Deadly Seduction

When A Stranger Calls

His Deadly Past

The Corkscrew Killer

First Responders: A spin-off from the NY State Troopers series

Playing With Fire

Private Conversation

The Right Groom

After The Fire

Caught In The Flames

Chasing The Fire

Legacy Series

Dark Legacy

Legacy of Lies

Secret Legacy

Emerald City

Investigate Away

Sail Away

Fly Away

Flirt Away

Colorado Brotherhood Protectors

Fighting For Esme

Defending Raven

Fay's Six

Darius' Promise

Yellowstone Brotherhood Protectors

Guarding Payton

Wyatt's Mission

Corbin's Mission

Candlewood Falls

Rivers Edge

The Buried Secret

Its In His Kiss

Lips Of An Angel

Kisses Sweeter than Wine

A Little Bit Whiskey

It's all in the Whiskey

Johnnie Walker

Georgia Moon

Jack Daniels

Jim Beam

Whiskey Sour

Whiskey Cobbler

Whiskey Smash

Irish Whiskey

The Monroes

Color Me Yours

Color Me Smart

Color Me Free

Color Me Lucky

Color Me Ice

Color Me Home

Search and Rescue

Protecting Ainsley

Protecting Clover

Protecting Olympia

Protecting Freedom

Protecting Princess

Protecting Marlowe

DELTA FORCE-NEXT GENERATION

Shielding Jolene

Shielding Aalyiah

Shielding Laine

Shielding Talullah

Shielding Maribel

Shielding Daisy

The Men of Thief Lake

Rekindled

Destiny's Dream

Federal Investigators

Jane Doe's Return

The Butterfly Murders

THE AEGIS NETWORK

The Sarich Brother

The Lighthouse

Her Last Hope

The Last Flight

The Return Home

The Matriarch

Aegis Network: Jacksonville Division

A SEAL's Honor

Talon's Honor

Arthur's Honor

Rex's Honor

Kent's Honor

Aegis Network Short Stories

Max & Milian

A Christmas Miracle

Spinning Wheels

Holiday's Vacation

The Brotherhood Protectors

Out of the Wild

Rough Justice

Rough Around The Edges

Rough Ride

Rough Edge

Rough Beauty

The Brotherhood Protectors

The Saving Series

Saving Love

Saving Magnolia

Saving Leather

Hot Hunks

Cove's Blind Date Blows Up

My Everyday Hero – Ledger

Tempting Tavor

Malachi's Mystic Assignment

Needing Neor

Holiday Romances

A Christmas Getaway

Alaskan Christmas

Whispers

Christmas In The Sand

Heroes & Heroines on the Field

Taking A Risk

Tee Time

A New Dawn

The Blind Date

Spring Fling

Summers Gone

Winter Wedding

The Awakening

The Collective Order

The Lost Sister

The Lost Soldier

The Lost Soul

The Lost Connection

The New Order

ABOUT THE AUTHOR

Jen Talty is the *USA Today* Bestselling Author of Contemporary Romance, Romantic Suspense, and Paranormal Romance. In the fall of 2020, her short story was selected and featured in a 1001 Dark Nights Anthology.

Regardless of the genre, her goal is to take you on a ride that will leave you floating under the sun with warmth in your heart. She writes stories about broken heroes and heroines who aren't necessarily looking for romance, but in the end, they find the kind of love books are written about :).

She first started writing while carting her kids to one hockey rink after the other, averaging 170 games per year between 3 kids in 2 countries and 5 states. Her first book, IN TWO WEEKS was originally published in 2007. In 2010 she helped form a publishing company (Cool Gus Publishing) with *NY Times* Bestselling Author Bob Mayer where she ran the technical side of the business through 2016.

Jen is currently enjoying the next phase of her life…the empty nester! She and her husband reside in Jupiter, Florida.

Grab a glass of vino, kick back, relax, and let the romance roll in…

Sign up for my Newsletter (https://dl.bookfunnel.com/82gm8b9k4y) where I often give away free books before publication.

Join my private Facebook group (https://www.facebook.com/groups/191706547909047/) where I post exclusive excerpts and discuss all things murder and love!

Never miss a new release. Follow me on Amazon:amazon.com/author/jentalty
And on Bookbub: bookbub.com/authors/jen-talty

There are many more books in this fan fiction world than listed here, for an up-to-date list go to www.AcesPress.com

You can also visit our Amazon page at: http://www.amazon.com/author/operationalpha

Special Forces: Operation Alpha World

Christie Adams: Charity's Heart
Elizabella Baker: Challenging Luke
Linzi Baxter: Dangerous Rescue
Misha Blake: Flash
Anna Blakely: Rescuing Gracelynn
Julia Bright: Saving Lorelei
Cara Carnes: Protecting Mari
Kendra Mei Chailyn: Beast
Melissa Kay Clarke: Rescuing Annabeth
Gia Cobie: Saved from Revenge
Samantha Cole: Handling Haven
KaLyn Cooper: Spring Unveiled
Jordan Dane: Redemption for Avery
D.M. Earl: Claire's Guardian
Riley Edwards: Protecting Olivia
Dorothy Ewels: Knight's Queen
Lila Ferrari: Protecting Joy
Nicole Flockton: Protecting Maria
Amy Gamet: Guarded by the SEAL
Lea Griffith: Finding Ava
Desiree Holt: Protecting Maddie

Danielle M. Haas: Crossroads of Betrayal
Bree Hera: Trusting the Team
Jesse Jacobson: Protecting Honor
Rayne Lewis: Justice for Mary
Ireland Lorelei: The Detective
Kristin Lynn: Worth the Risk
JM Madden: Rescuing Olivia
A.M. Mahler: Griffin
Ellie Masters: Sybil's Protector
Trish McCallan: Hero Under Fire
Naomi McKay: Twist
Rachel McNeely: The SEAL's Surprise Baby
KD Michaels: Saving Laura
Olivia Michaels: Protecting Harper
Annie Miller: Securing Willow
MJ Nightingale: Protecting Beauty
C.K. O'Connor: Delaney's Bodyguard
Melinda Owens: Betraying Katie
Victoria Paige: Reclaiming Izabel
Danielle Pays: Defending Sarina
Lainey Reese: Protecting New York
KeKe Renée: Protecting Bria
Taryn Rivers: Savage Cove
TL Reeve and Michele Ryan: Extracting Mateo
Ariana Rose: Chasing Paige
Deanna L. Rowley: Saving Veronica
Angela Rush: Charlotte
E.M. Shue: Discovering Tyler
Rose Smith: Saving Satin

Tyler Anne Snell: Cowboy Heat
Dee Stewart: Fighting for Brielle
Lynne St. James: SEAL's Spitfire
Bella Stone: Rexar
Jen Talty: Protecting Ainsley
Reina Torres, Rescuing Hi'ilani
LJ Vickery: Circus Comes to Town
R. C. Wynne: Shadows Renewed

Delta Team Three Series

Lori Ryan: Nori's Delta
Becca Jameson: Destiny's Delta
Lynne St James, Gwen's Delta
Elle James: Ivy's Delta
Riley Edwards: Hope's Delta

Police and Fire: Operation Alpha World

Freya Barker: Burning for Autumn
B.P. Beth: Scott
Jane Blythe: Salvaging Marigold
Julia Bright: Justice for Amber
Gia Cobie: Saved from Revenge
Hadley Finn: Exton
Danielle M. Haas: Crossroads of Betrayal
Deanndra Hall: Shelter for Sharla
Jenna Harte: Dead But Not Forgotten
India Kells: Game Master
Amber Kuhlman: Protecting Paisley
Reina Torres: Justice for Sloane

Aubree Valentine, Justice for Danielle

Tarpley VFD Series

Silver James, Fighting for Elena
Deanndra Hall, Fighting for Carly
Haven Rose, Fighting for Calliope
MJ Nightingale, Fighting for Jemma
TL Reeve, Fighting for Brittney
Nicole Flockton, Fighting for Nadia

As you know, this book included at least one character from Susan Stoker's books. To check out more, see below.

<u>SEAL of Protection: Alliance Series</u>

Protecting Remi

Protecting Wren (Nov 5, 2024)

Protecting Josie (Mar 4, 2025)

Protecting Maggie (Apr 1, 2025)

Protecting Addison (May 6, 2025)

Protecting Kelli (TBA)

Protecting Bree (TBA)

<u>The Refuge Series</u>

Deserving Alaska

Deserving Henley

Deserving Reese

Deserving Cora

Deserving Lara

Deserving Maisy (Oct 1, 2024)

Deserving Ryleigh (Jan 7, 2025)

<u>SEAL Team Hawaii Series</u>

Finding Elodie

Finding Lexie

Finding Kenna

Finding Monica

Finding Carly

Finding Ashlyn
Finding Jodelle

Eagle Point Search & Rescue

Searching for Lilly
Searching for Elsie
Searching for Bristol
Searching for Caryn
Searching for Finley
Searching for Heather
Searching for Khloe

Delta Team Two Series

Shielding Gillian
Shielding Kinley
Shielding Aspen
Shielding Jayme (novella)
Shielding Riley
Shielding Devyn
Shielding Ember
Shielding Sierra

SEAL of Protection: Legacy Series

Securing Caite (FREE!)
Securing Brenae (novella)
Securing Sidney
Securing Piper
Securing Zoey

Securing Avery
Securing Kalee
Securing Jane

Delta Force Heroes Series

Rescuing Rayne (FREE!)
Rescuing Aimee (novella)
Rescuing Emily
Rescuing Harley
Marrying Emily (novella)
Rescuing Kassie
Rescuing Bryn
Rescuing Casey
Rescuing Sadie (novella)
Rescuing Wendy
Rescuing Mary
Rescuing Macie (novella)
Rescuing Annie

Badge of Honor: Texas Heroes Series

Justice for Mackenzie (FREE!)
Justice for Mickie
Justice for Corrie
Justice for Laine (novella)
Shelter for Elizabeth
Justice for Boone
Shelter for Adeline
Shelter for Sophie

Justice for Erin
Justice for Milena
Shelter for Blythe
Justice for Hope
Shelter for Quinn
Shelter for Koren
Shelter for Penelope

SEAL of Protection Series

Protecting Caroline (FREE!)
Protecting Alabama
Protecting Fiona
Marrying Caroline (novella)
Protecting Summer
Protecting Cheyenne
Protecting Jessyka
Protecting Julie (novella)
Protecting Melody
Protecting the Future
Protecting Kiera (novella)
Protecting Alabama's Kids (novella)
Protecting Dakota

New York Times, USA Today and *Wall Street Journal* Bestselling Author Susan Stoker has a heart as big as the state of Tennessee where she lives, but this all American girl has also spent the last fourteen years living in Missouri, California, Colorado, Indiana, and

Texas. She's married to a retired Army man who now gets to follow *her* around the country.

www.stokeraces.com
www.AcesPress.com
susan@stokeraces.com

Made in United States
Cleveland, OH
09 June 2025